Ghosts of Florida's Gulf Coast

Alan Brown

Pineapple Press, Inc.
Sarasota, Florida

Inquiries should be addressed to:
Pineapple Press, Inc.
P.O. Box 3889
Sarasota, Florida 34230

www.pineapplepress.com

Library of Congress Cataloging-in-Publication Data

Brown, Alan.
Ghosts of Florida's Gulf Coast / Alan Brown.
    pagescm
Includes bibliographical references and index.
ISBN 978-1-56164-721-7 (pbk.)
1. Haunted places—Florida—Gulf Coast. 2. Ghosts—Florida—Gulf Coast. I. Title.

BF1472.U6B7423 2014
133.109759—dc23

2014012297

First Edition

Design by Jennifer Borresen

Table of Contents

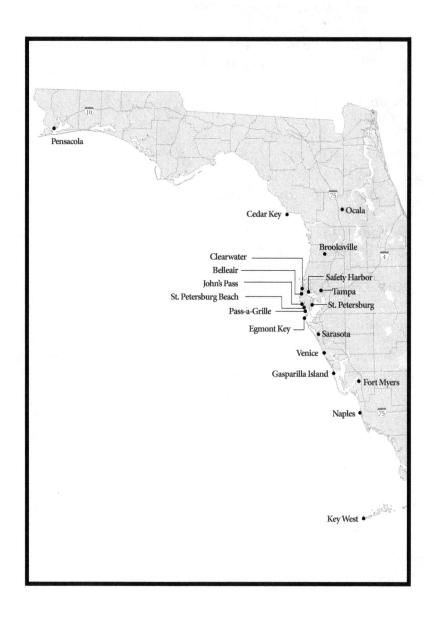

Pensacola

Cedar Key •   • Ocala

Brooksville •

Clearwater ————
Belleair ————
John's Pass ————
St. Petersburg Beach ————   Safety Harbor
Pass-a-Grille ————   Tampa
Egmont Key ————   St. Petersburg

• Sarasota

Venice •

Gasparilla Island •   • Fort Myers

Naples •

Key West •

Introduction

Thanks to its various depictions in the media, Florida's Gulf Coast seems to be a very familiar place to most Americans, even if they have never been there. To many people, the Gulf Coast is a seafood-lover's paradise where you can dine on freshly caught shrimp and lobsters. To others, the Gulf Coast is a breeding ground for an abundance of aquatic birds and mammals. History enthusiasts appreciate the Civil War-era and Spanish-American War-era masonry forts that dot the shoreline. Lighthouse lovers dream of visiting places like Pensacola Lighthouse, where mighty nineteenth-century beacons still stand. Vacationers are attracted to the laid-back lifestyle of Gulf Coast residents, an image popularized by entertainers like Jimmy Buffet. And people interested in the paranormal explore the region's dark side.

Ghost stories, it turns out, are as much an integral part of the Gulf Coast as are palm trees, pelicans, and pounding surf. The first inhabitants of this area, the Native Americans, left an indelible imprint on its place names, on its landscape, and, some say, on its spirit energy. The natural and man-made catastrophes that have wreaked havoc on Florida's Gulf Coast for thousands of years have also contributed to the Gulf's haunted reputation. The spirits of Civil War soldiers, as well as of hundreds of refugees and escaped slaves who fled to Florida during the conflict, populate many of the state's ghost legends. Massive hurricanes that have claimed scores of lives and even changed the very shoreline figure prominently in the ghost stories of the Gulf Coast.

Ghost stories do more than simply commemorate the suffering and heroism of Florida's Gulf Coast residents. They also reflect the Gulf's romantic allure, produced largely by the region's tropical climate and beauty. In some of the Gulf's oldest legends, pirates like Gasparilla still prowl the coastline in search of plunder. Depression-era gangsters like Al Capone still conduct their nefarious activities in Florida's bays and inlets. Even some of the legends of baseball's Golden Age, such as Babe Ruth and Lou Gehrig, have found the sunny shores of the Gulf Coast difficult to leave. The Gulf Coast is an otherworldly place, a realm where the long-dead past has found new life in ghost tales and, sometimes, in the here and now. The inhabitants of Gulf Coast towns and cities have not only learned to live harmoniously with previous residents, but they also take pride in the Gulf Coast's reputation as a storied place. A plethora of pirate festivals, Civil War reenactments, and ghost tours testify to this fact.

Chapter One

Belleair

The Belleview-Biltmore Hotel

The Belleview-Biltmore Hotel was built in 1897 by Florida developer and railroad tycoon Henry Plant, whose other architectural creations include the stunning 1891 Tampa Bay Hotel, now the Henry Plant Museum and part of the University of Tampa. Plant erected the Belleview-Biltmore to accommodate the passengers on his railroad line serving the west coast of Florida. The largest wooden building in Florida, the hotel is noteworthy for its green, sloped roof and hand-carved woodwork. The 82,000-square-foot building was the centerpiece of a 160-acre resort that included a beach club, restaurant, golf course, and swimming pool.

The Belleview-Biltmore was a luxury hotel in every sense of the word. Guests were treated to such amenities as shoe shining and stained-glass ceilings. The hotel's guestbook included some of the twentieth century's best-known celebrities, including Thomas Edison, Margaret Thatcher, the Duke of Windsor, Babe Ruth, and Joe DiMaggio. The U.S. government appropriated the hotel during World War II, but after the war, the resort regained its reputation as the playground for the rich and famous, attracting the likes of presidents—Gerald Ford, Jimmy Carter, George H.W. Bush, and Barack Obama—and rock stars. In 1976 members of

Bob Dylan's Rolling Thunder Revue played two shows in the Starlight Ballroom.

Today the hotel's biggest draw is its paranormal activity, not its elegant accommodations. The subjects of one of the hotel's signature ghost stories are a bride and groom who booked the bridal suite, Room 4336, for their honeymoon in 1922. The day before the wedding, the groom drove to Tampa for a bachelor party. The next day, the bride, known today as "Annie," was trying on her wedding dress when she was interrupted by a knock on the door and opened it to find the manager and two hotel staff members. In a low, solemn voice, the manager informed the young woman that her fiancé had been killed in an automobile accident that morning. The grief-stricken bride-to-be walked out to the balcony and jumped to her death. Ever since her tragic death, the filmy image of a woman has been seen on several of the balconies. In addition, the specter of a woman dressed in a bridal gown has been reported walking down the hallways on the upper floors.

The Biltmore's best-known ghost is the spirit of Morton Plant's wife, Maisie, Henry Plant's daughter-in-law. In 1916 Morton gave Maisie a string of pearls designed by Pierre Cartier himself. Maisie had not owned the pearls for very long before she lost them. Maisie, Morton, and the hotel staff combed the entire hotel but were unable to locate the pearls, which were worth $1.2 million. No one has ever found them. Legend has it that Maisie's ghost is still wandering the hallways and checking rooms in search of her lost pearls.

The ghosts in the Belleview-Biltmore Hotel have been known to manifest themselves in other ways as well. Many people have reported hearing sighs and moans in the hallways and rooms. Elevators ride up and down when no one is inside. Some people have caught a glimpse of the specter of a tall, dark man inside the elevator. Doors open and close by themselves. Members of the kitchen staff claim to have heard the banging of pots and pans when they are all alone. Greg Jenkins, author of *Florida's Ghostly Legends and Haunted Folklore*, says that in one of the unused rooms on the fifth floor, an old rotary phone that has been in the room since the 1920s occasionally rings in the middle of the night. The phone's ringing is particularly unnerving because the cord has been removed. Staff members who have answered the phone have been startled to hear heavy breathing on the line.

The hotel closed in 2009, and rumors soon spread that the new owners, BB Hotel LLC, were planning to renovate the structure. However, in 2013 BB Hotel proposed a plan to raze the historic building to make room for townhouses and condominiums. Not surprisingly, a large group of citizens have protested the destruction of the last of Henry Plant's hotels in existence. An investment group called Belleair Biltmore Partners announced in 2013 that it had raised the money to purchase the hotel, but the fate of the Belleview-Biltmore is still up in the air. If it is eventually replaced by condominiums, chances are good that the displaced spirits will simply move into their new residence.

Chapter Two

Brooksville

The May-Stringer House (Brooksville Heritage Museum)

The May-Stringer House was built by Brooksville pioneer John May. The two-story, four-room house was one of the first houses built under the Florida Settlers Act, which gave settlers 160 acres as long as they lived on the land. After John May died, his widow, Marena, married John Saxon. In 1869 Marena died while giving birth to a daughter, Jessie May, who died three years later.

The home's next owner was Dr. Stringer, who redesigned the house in the Queen Anne style. He added a tower, a three-bay façade, and a wraparound porch so he would have the largest house in town. A fan of Nathaniel Hawthorne, Dr. Stringer also added seven gables as an homage to one of his favorite novels, *House of the Seven Gables*. After Dr. Stringer and his family moved out, the house was abandoned, and looters and years of neglect took a heavy toll on the once-fine home. It was saved from utter ruin by the city of Brooksville, which restored the house and reopened it as the Brooksville Heritage Museum. The May-Stringer house is now one of the best-preserved examples of the Queen Anne style in Hernando County, and it contains displays from the area's past in the doctor's room, the telephone/telegraph room, and a war room.

The ghostly goings-on in the May-Stringer House probably spring from the home's close association with death. Not only did John May, Marena, and her son and daughter die in the house, so did a number of Dr. Stringer's patients. The house served as a sanitarium for terminally ill patients suffering from yellow fellow, smallpox, scarlet fever, and other epidemics. Legend has it that a soldier who returned to Brooksville from Europe after World War I discovered that his fiancée had married someone else in his absence. The soldier who had endured so much pain and suffering could take no more. He hanged himself in the master bedroom.

The ghostly activity in the old museum has manifested in a number of ways over the years. Docents have seen spectral forms floating through dark hallways and mists that suddenly appear. Some staff members have encountered sudden cold spots throughout the house. Glowing orbs have appeared above the home's tin roof. Bonnie Le Tourneau, a weekend volunteer guide, said she once felt someone touch her shoulder when she was alone in the house. She has also heard footsteps on the upper floors of the house. The docents estimate that nine ghosts may be haunting the May-Stringer House.

The ghost presumed to be responsible for much of the paranormal activity is the ghost of John May's three-year-old daughter, Jessie May, whose mother died in childbirth. Some staff members believe the little girl missed her mother so much that she died of a broken heart. Late one afternoon, Bonnie Le Tourneau heard the faint cries of a child she believes was Jessie May. Virginia Jackson, director of the Hernando County Historical Society, told Jack Powell, author of *Haunting Sunshine*, this story. One day while cleaning the house, she unplugged the vacuum cleaner so she could move to a different room. In the ensuing silence, she heard a little girl crying,

"Mama! Mama!" The pathetic little voice seemed to be coming from the attic. Jackson plugged in the vacuum cleaner and resumed her cleaning. When she unplugged it a second time, she heard the child's voice again. She checked the attic, but no one was there. Jackson later discovered that two workmen had also heard the little girl's voice and refused to reenter the house. A third workman who was cutting wood with an electric saw heard "Mama! Mama!" every time he turned off the saw.

Despite her melancholy voice, Jessie May has a playful side. Docents opening the museum in the morning have discovered some of the home's antique wooden toys moved around, sometimes to different rooms. Jessie May seems to enjoy moving a pair of century-old baby shoes to a particular chair during the night. She also rearranges objects in the schoolroom and in her playroom on the second floor. Lights sometimes come on inside the house hours after it has been locked for the night.

Unlike at some historic homes, staff members at the May-Stringer House are proud of the museum's haunted reputation. In fact, they openly advertise that the house has been certified as haunted by several paranormal research groups. Being designated one of Florida's paranormal hot spots by groups like Florida Ghost Hunters and Paranormal Seekers is a good thing, as far as the docents are concerned. The museum even offers ghost tours by appointment. A guide begins the tour by leading visitors through the house and pointing out where most of the paranormal activity occurs. After explaining the history of the house and revealing some of the ghost stories, she then gives the visitors ghost-hunting advice and lets them wander through the house on their own. Visitors are encouraged to bring ghost-hunting equipment, such as digital voice recorders, EMF detectors, and digital cameras.

Chapter Three
_____

Cedar Key

Island Hotel and Restaurant

Most tourists view today's Cedar Key as an idyllic refuge from the fast pace of Florida's mainland. In 1859 when Major John Parsons bought the land on which the Island Hotel and Restaurant now stands, however, he believed that the completion of the Florida Railroad would transform the sleepy little island into a bustling metropolis. By 1860 the building that would become Parsons and Hale's General Store was completed. The structure has survived floods, fires, and hurricanes, due in large part to its ten-inch-thick walls and the twelve-inch-thick oak beams that form the framework. Parsons and his partner, Francis E. Hale, were in business a little more than a year when the Civil War destroyed their dream of financial success. Union troops burned down every building on Cedar Key except for Parsons and Hale's General Store, which they used as a barracks. After Confederate troops regained control of Cedar Key, they too quartered at the store.

Parsons and Hale continued to operate a store from the building throughout the remainder of the nineteenth century. In 1896 the town was slammed by a fierce hurricane and nearly destroyed by a raging fire soon afterward. Parsons and Hale's General Store suffered considerable damage in the hurricane. After Francis Hale died in 1910, his business partner's son, Langdon Parsons, sold the store. For the next few years, the building served as the post office and the customs house. Then in 1915, Simon Feinberg purchased the building and converted it to the Bay Hotel. He repaired the stairway and added the second-floor balcony. Following Feinberg's untimely demise in 1919, a number of different people owned the hotel, including Mrs. Wilda Finlayson, who operated a millinery store on the first floor during the 1920s. A man named Crittendon turned the building into a speakeasy and "house of ill repute" in the 1930s.

The fortunes of the hotel, like those of the other businesses on Cedar Key, took a downward turn during the Depression, especially after the wooden bridges were washed out and the railroad ceased its run to the island in 1932. The hotel caught fire three times in the 1930s, and authorities suspected arson. The Andrews family acquired the hotel in the late 1930s, and between 1941 and 1945, Forest and Nettie Andrews operated the hotel, which by this time had become dilapidated.

The hotel's saviors after World War II were Bessie and Loyal "Gibby" Gibbs, who became the new owners in 1946. The couple renamed the hotel the Island Hotel and commissioned local painter Helen Parramore to paint King Neptune and a couple of sea nymphs. The painting hung on the wall behind the bar, which came to be known as the Neptune Bar. Bessie also set about establishing the Island Hotel as the place to go on Cedar Key for seafood. The restaurant featured dishes prepared by Bessie and her cook, Catherine Johnson.

The hotel suffered a temporary setback in 1950 when a hurricane blew the roof off the building, drenching the upstairs rooms. Bessie continued running the hotel after Gibby died in 1962, but excruciating arthritis pain forced her to sell the hotel in 1973 to Charlie and Shirley English, who, in turn, sold the establishment to Harold Nabors. In the late 1970s, Nabors focused his attention on the bar and the newly added annex garden.

The hotel enjoyed a resurgence of popularity under the ownership of Marcia Rogers in the 1980s. Jimmy Buffett, a frequent guest, performed in the Neptune Bar. Marcia restored the restaurant's reputation for fine Florida cuisine. The only serious mistake Rogers made was to convert the Neptune Bar into a coffee and juice bar. Locals were so outraged that they burned her in effigy in front of the post office.

In 1992 Marcia Rogers sold the bar to Tom and Allison Sanders, who hired a local carpenter to rebuild the bar. They also removed the portrait of Neptune and turned it over to restoration expert Katrina Blumenstein. Behind the painting, Tom found several bullet holes, confirming rumors that a drunken guest had once fired a pistol at Neptune. New items on Chef Jahn McCumber's menu attracted more customers to the restaurant. Before long, the Island Hotel had once more become the social hub of Cedar Key.

In 1996 Tom and Allison Sanders sold the hotel to Dawn Fisher and Tony Cousins, who immediately began adding their own personal touches to the hotel. They replaced the jalousie windows with new timber sash windows, restored the conference room, and refurbished the three bedrooms on the first floor. The couple also restored the dining room to its 1940s' appearance. In 1998, Dawn and Tony found time to get married.

The strain of raising a family and running a hotel eventually proved to be too much for Dawn and Tony. They sold the hotel in 2001 to Marylou and Bill Stewart but returned as receivers a year later when the Stewarts fired the staff and closed the hotel. The Cousins were able to rehire most of the former staff, who were eager to work for them again. In 2004 Dawn and Tony sold the hotel to current owners Andy Blair and his wife, Stanley. The Blairs breathed new life into the old hotel, repainting the lobby and buying new furniture. They have also done their part to keep the hotel's ghost stories alive.

A group of paranormal investigators who visited the Island Hotel several years ago concluded that thirteen spirits were still in the building. The oldest of the hotel's ghost stories revolves around a nine-year-old African-American boy who was hired by the manager of the general store during the Civil War to sweep the floors and stock the shelves. One day the manager saw the boy put something in his pocket as he walked through the store. Assuming that the boy was pilfering merchandise, the manager ran after him. Either the boy was too fast or the manager was too slow, but the child was never apprehended. Nor was he ever seen again. The mystery of the boy's disappearance was solved a year later when workmen draining a cistern in the basement of the store discovered the bones of a little boy. The authorities assumed that he had accidentally fallen into the cistern while trying to escape from the irate store manager. Staff members bold enough to walk downstairs to the basement claim to have seen the crouching form of the little boy, huddling in the shadows in the hope of avoiding the wrath of the store manager.

The Civil War also produced one of the Island Hotel's ghost stories. Many guests have seen the spirit of a Confederate sentry standing guard just inside the doors leading to the balcony on the second floor. The apparition is visible for just a few seconds before it vanishes. I attempted to determine the validity of this tale when my wife, Marilyn, and I stayed at the Island Hotel a couple of years ago. I was planning to scan the area in front of the balcony doors at sunrise the next day, but I was curious to see if perhaps the spirit was active in the evening as well. At 7:30 P.M., Marilyn and I stood in front of the balcony doors. She scanned the front of the doors with an EMF meter but detected no disturbances in the electromagnetic field. After she was finished, I scanned the same area with my K-II meter. When I passed the K-II over the left side of the

The Island Hotel is haunted by the ghost of Simon Feinberg, who died of food poisoning there.

doors, the meter registered light green and yellow and for a few seconds spiked all the way to red. I then scanned the right side of the door, but the K-II registered no activity at all. When I moved it back to the left side of the door, the lights began flashing again. When the red light appeared, I experienced a tingling sensation in the little finger of the hand holding the K-II meter. The next morning, I scanned the balcony doors again but detected no fluctuations in the electromagnetic field on either side.

Simon Feinberg's spirit seems reluctant to surrender control of the hotel to the present owners. Legend has it that

Feinberg, a teetotaler, was displeased with the surreptitious business ventures of his manager, who had set up a whiskey still in the attic. When Feinberg informed the manager that he would have to dismantle his illegal distillery, instead of protesting, the manager apologized and offered to make dinner for his boss. Feinberg agreed and enjoyed a sumptuous meal. He retired for the night soon afterward but never woke up. The next morning, the local physician determined that Simon Feinberg had died of food poisoning. The discovery of a piece of copper pipe by Harold Nabors in a false roof twelve inches below the annex roof lends an air of truth to this story. Over the years, many guests and staff members have encountered Simon Feinberg's ghost wandering the hallways, usually at night.

One of the other former owners of the Island Hotel has also found it difficult to leave. Bessie Gibbs' ghost is probably an active presence in the hotel because it was her home for twenty-six years. She is a mischievous spirit who rearranges furniture and closes doors. She has even been credited with locking guests out of their rooms. A few guests swear that Bessie Gibbs' ghost passed through the door of their room and exited through the rear wall. During a séance held at the hotel, a medium asserted that Bessie's ghost is still residing in her bedroom, Room 29.

Another victim of foul play haunts the Island Hotel. This particular ghost is the spirit of a prostitute who was murdered by a dissatisfied customer when the hotel was a brothel in the 1930s. She is an affectionate apparition who disrupts the sleep of male guests in Rooms 27 and 28. A guest typically wakes up to see an attractive young woman sitting on the edge of his bed. She bends down, kisses him, and vanishes.

The popularity of the Island Hotel's ghost stories

prompted local newspaper reporter Rick Burnham to spend the night in one of the rooms with a friend. Burnham was hoping to be awakened by the spectral knocking on the door that staff members had told him about. He wasn't disappointed. Burnham was fast asleep when he heard someone knocking on the door. He shook his friend awake and asked him if he had heard anything, but he said no. Burnham tried to go back to sleep. A few minutes later, he heard the knocking again. This time he rushed to the door and flung it open. No one was there.

The next day, Burnham drove to the Wal-Mart in Chiefland. When he returned to his room at the Island Hotel later that evening, he set the bag containing his purchases on the floor. That night he was awakened by the sound of someone rifling though the plastic Wal-Mart bag. He turned on the light and looked around the room. He was totally alone.

Stanley Blair, current owner of the Island Hotel, receives inquiries about the ghosts at least two or three times a week. Stanley's most memorable paranormal experience took place one evening in September 2011 when she walked into the dining room and found a knife on the floor. "I became very angry," Stanley said. "I thought to myself, *how many of our wait staff walked past that knife and didn't pick it up?*" She went back into the kitchen and talked to the waitresses. When Stanley returned to the dining room, a diner waved her over and said, "I want you to know that I watched that knife jump off the table."

Two years earlier, a woman staying in Room 33, where Simon Feinberg died, told Stanley that the night she checked in, she was overcome with a feeling of dread in her room. She sensed that she was not alone. As she gazed around the room nervously, she recalled her mother's words: "Anytime you are frightened or worried, just say the Rosary." She climbed into bed and began saying the Rosary with the lights on. Suddenly, she heard a ghostly male voice say, "Shh! Shh!" The woman was convinced that the spirit did not want to hear the clacking of her Rosary beads. The fact that Simon Feinberg was Jewish could have something to do with his reaction toward the woman's prayers.

Stanley's husband, Andy, believes a number of strange events have occurred in the old hotel that could be supernatural in origin. "Sometimes things move around," Andy says. "Wet footprints appear on the hallway floor. It looks like someone has just gotten out of the shower. I walked into the dining room one morning and it smelled like a wet dog had just walked into the room. There were no dogs in the hotel at the time."

The Island Hotel and Restaurant continues to attract famous people just as it did in the 1940s and 1950s, when notables such as Tennessee Ernie Ford, Myrna Loy, Pearl Buck, and Richard Boone basked in the beauty of Cedar Key's tropical surroundings. The most interesting guests, however, are the ones who remain at the hotel long after their allotted time on earth has passed. From the perspective of a lover of the paranormal, the presence of ghosts at the Island Hotel and Restaurant more than makes up for the absence of amenities such as telephones and televisions.

Chapter Four

Clearwater

Robert L.F. Sikes Public Library

Clearwater's public library has undergone a
number of different incarnations since Bertha
Henry established a library in her home on
East Pine Avenue in the 1940s. A few years later, she moved
the library to the Episcopal Church. It was then moved to a
small home on West Highway 90. After the Women's Club of
Clearwater took over the library, it was moved to an apartment
on East Woodruff Avenue. When its collection became too
large for its small quarters, it was moved to a shopping center
on Highway 90. In 1976 the library was moved into a brand-
new building near Twin Hills Park. The Robert L.F. Sikes
Public library, as it was now known, remained at this location
until 1993, when the City of Clearwater sold it to Okaloosa
Walton Community College, which is now Northwest Florida
State College. The library was finally moved to its present
location off North Highway 85 at 1445 Commerce Drive. Its
namesake, Robert L.F. Sikes, had a strong personal connection
to the Highway 90 building, which, some librarians say,
outlived him.

Robert L.F. Sikes was one of Clearwater's most
popular congressmen. He was first elected as a Democrat to
the Seventy-seventh and Seventy-eighth Congresses in the
spring of 1941. After serving as a major in World War II, he
was elected to the Seventy-ninth and the sixteen succeeding

Congresses between 1945 and 1978. In 1976 Sikes was accused by a lobbying group of a conflict of interest after he promoted the establishment of the Pensacola Naval Air Station bank, which he owned stock in. On July 26, 1976, Sikes was officially reprimanded by the House of Representatives for financial misconduct. He decided not to run for reelection in 1978.

Sikes died on September 28, 1994. "Uncle Bob," as the staff called him, was a personable man and a strong supporter of the library, on the second floor of which he had offices. His fondness for the library seems to have lingered after his death. Soon afterward, some people claimed to have seen him walking down the hallways. One librarian who had a personal encounter with the spirit of Robert L. F. Sikes was Sharon Sutton, who worked at the library between 1995 and 2007. One evening just before 8:00 P.M., Sharon and another librarian were the only ones in the building. "Anna was in the Children's Room, and I was standing at the main desk," recalls Sharon. "Suddenly a voice behind me said, 'Hey!' I looked around and no one was there. I called out to Anna and told her what had happened. Anna said jokingly, 'Maybe it was the ghost of Uncle Bob. He likes to pay us a visit now and then, you know.'"

Sharon has not heard of any ghostly activity inside the former library now that it is being used as classroom space. Perhaps the boisterousness of the students has disrupted the quiet environment that "Uncle Bob" seems to prefer.

The Royalty Theater

In 1920 Senator-Elect John S. Taylor began construction of a new theater at 405 Cleveland Street. However, storm damage forced construction workers to start all over again. The Capitol Theater finally opened in 1921 as a venue for vaudeville and opera. With its 500-plus seating capacity and its excellent natural acoustics, the Capitol became known as one of the finest theaters in the entire state. By the 1930s, the Capitol featured movies during the week and vaudeville acts on Friday nights. During World War II, the theater hosted Air Force and Marine troops. For the next three decades, the Capitol was known as the city's best movie theater. The building was renovated in 1962, but in the 1970s the crowds began to decline. In 1979 the theater's managing company, Pitt Southern, decided not to renew its contract. The new manager, Bill Neville, tried to revive the old theater's popularity by showing classic films at cheap prices, but the expected crowds did not materialize and the Capitol Theater closed its doors in 1980. In 1981 a local theater group leased and remodeled the old building and reopened it as the Royalty Theater. In 1996 the owners sold the building for $132,000. In 1999 the theater was rescued from destruction, this time by Socrates Charos, who bought the building for $250,000. A $3.8-million renovation project breathed new life into the Royalty Theater, but Charos lost the theater to foreclosure in 2008. One year later, the city of Clearwater purchased the theater and reduced its seating capacity to 433. Today the Royalty Theater hosts live concerts, musical performances, plays, and independent and classic movies.

A number of famous people have graced the stage of the Royalty Theater throughout its long history, including Dean Martin, Frank Sinatra, Elvis Presley, Liza Minnelli, Bob Hope, and Sammy Davis Jr. Today the theater has gained notoriety for appearances of a far different sort.

The first ghost to make its presence known in the theater was the spirit of Bill Neville. In the early 1980s, his battered body was found in the balcony area. Neville had been robbed of seven dollars and change. The wounds inflicted on the corpse were so severe that Neville appeared to have been the victim of a hate crime. Rumors soon spread that his effeminate mannerisms had inflamed the anger of a couple of drunken gay-bashers.

Reports of strange occurrences began surfacing not long after Neville's death. He is said to be a protective spirit who saved the life of an electrician who tripped over an extension cord while working on the balcony. Just before he fell over the edge of the balcony, the man felt someone grab his shoulders and pull him back to safety. The electrician turned to thank the person he thought was standing behind him, but no one was there. Neville's spirit could also be the invisible presence that prevented a suspicious-looking man from opening the front door. He fled when he looked through the window and saw Charos walking toward the door. Charos, who had no trouble opening the door, suspects that the stranger had come to the theater with bad intentions, possibly robbery or murder.

Another of the theater's ghosts is the spirit of a sea captain. Charos first encountered this apparition in the early 2000s while working by himself late one night. He happened to look up and saw a strange man standing in the doorway. The man was wearing a dark blue coat and a fisherman's cap. The specter's face was so clear that Charos could see his blue eyes and goatee. The amiable figure walked up to Charos and shook his hand. Then the man did something totally unexpected. "The ghost walked through me and went into the theater," Charos said. "What an introduction!" Before the spirit dematerialized, Charos noticed that he had no legs. Not long after Charos' sighting, women walking through the theater complained about being groped about the legs and buttocks by an invisible hand. The sea captain's ghost has also been known to disrupt performances by making banging noises.

The ghost of a little girl has also been seen at the theater. Her true identity is unknown, but staff members call her Angelica or Angelina. She is thought to be one of the children who died in one of Clearwater's influenza or yellow fever outbreaks. The playful little specter was first seen in the 1960s, not long after workmen began repairing storm damage to the theater. Witnesses described her as a ten-year-old girl in a blue, yellow, or green dress who spins and dances on the stage. Everyone who has seen her says she has a bright smile on her face gives the impression that she is happy to be spending eternity at the Royalty Theater.

Much of the paranormal activity observed in the theater cannot be attributed to a specific spirit. One ghost seems to express its musical preferences by turning the lights off and on. Socrates Charos, who referred to the theater's ghosts as "angels," said that one day the piano tuner had just entered the theater when the lights turned on. After he had completed the job, he thanked Charos for turning the lights on for him. Surprised, Charos stared at the piano tuner for a few seconds before replying that he had just arrived at the theater a few minutes earlier. Similar incidents confirmed Charos' suspicions that the ghost liked piano music better than any other kind, especially rock. One afternoon, several actors began playing heavy metal on the radio. Immediately, the lights went off. The lights came back on only after the last of the actors left the theater. Not long thereafter, workmen who were making repairs in the old building decided to switch the channel on their radio to a heavy metal station. Charos asked one of the men to turn the volume down but he refused. A few minutes later, the plastic sheets covering several of the chairs flew up all the way to the ceiling. The workers were then more than happy to lower the radio's volume.

Charos' "angels" did other strange things too. Alarms often went off by themselves, usually on Saturday mornings. Visitors have detected the unmistakable aroma of freshly baked chocolate chip cookies. Not long after acquiring the old theater, Charos discovered that the spirits liked some colors more than others. Workmen had just finished painting the ceiling blue when Charos noticed that none of the electrical equipment worked. Suspecting that at least one of the theater's ghosts hated blue, he instructed the workmen to repaint the ceiling gold. As soon as they were finished, the equipment worked perfectly. The spirits' dislike of blue paint is supported by the nineteenth-century folk belief that painting the shutters of a house blue repels ghosts.

Evidence of paranormal activity at the Royalty in the form of orbs, mists, and ectoplasm has been collected over the years. In December 2001, the Central Florida Ghost Team conducted a formal paranormal investigation of the theater. Two orbs were captured on a 35mm camera in the balcony where Bill Neville's corpse was found. Two members smelled flowers near the building's entrance. In one of the electronic voice phenomena (EVP) recordings that night, a spectral voice identified itself as Angelica. A foglike image hovering over the door to the restroom from the girls' dressing room appeared in both a digital photo and a video. Throughout the investigation, the batteries in several of the group's cameras were drained. The group concluded that the theater is definitely haunted.

Chapter Five

Egmont Key

Egmont Key State Park

E gmont Key is a small island located just inside the mouth of Tampa Bay. In 1761 the English took control of the key and named it after the Earl of Egmont. Egmont Key continued to change hands between the Spanish and the British until the United States claimed it in 1827. Because a number of ships were foundering on the sandbars surrounding Egmont Key in the 1830s and 1840s, plans were made for the construction of a lighthouse in 1847. Construction of the forty-foot-tall brick lighthouse was completed in 1848, but a hurricane in September of that year severely damaged the lighthouse and submerged the island under six feet of water. The lighthouse keeper, Sherrod Edwards, rowed to Tampa in a small boat with his family and never returned. When another hurricane ravaged Egmont Key in 1852, the lighthouse was damaged beyond repair.

The lighthouse was rebuilt in 1857 with funds allocated by Congress. The eighty-seven-foot-tall light was outfitted with an Argard-class kerosene lamp and a third-order Fresnel lens. During the Civil War, Confederate forces briefly took control of Egmont Key and removed the Fresnel lens to vex the Union navy's efforts to blockade Tampa Bay. The lens was reinstalled after the war and a new lighthouse keeper and his assistant lived on Egmont Key with their families between 1866 and 1898.

In 1898, during the Spanish-American War, Fort Dade was constructed as part of the United States' coastal defense system. By 1906 a community of three hundred servicemen and their families were living at Fort Dade. The community had many of the features of a typical small town around the turn of the century, including red-brick streets, electricity, a hospital, a cafeteria-style dining hall, and a cemetery. When the Spanish-American War ended, most of the servicemen returned to the mainland, leaving only a few soldiers behind. The military abandoned Egmont Key completely in 1923.

The storms and hurricanes that have buffeted Egmont Key since the armed forces abandoned it reduced a number of the abandoned buildings to ruins. In 1974 Egmont Key was taken over by the U.S. Fish and Wildlife Service. In 1989 the lighthouse became fully automated, eliminating the need for a lighthouse keeper. That same year, Egmont Key was added to the National Registry of Historic Places. Today much of the little island has been taken over by trees and bushes, nesting sea turtles, and ghosts.

Most of the sightings at Egmont Key occur at twilight and just before dawn. Visitors and park rangers have reported hearing the sounds of someone running among the ruins. They have also heard spectral voices and seen faint lights from the spot where the lighthouse keeper's residence once stood. People have also seen dark figures creeping around the foundations of the old buildings.

In the book *Florida's Ghostly Legends and Haunted Folklore*, Volume 3, a park ranger told author Greg Jenkins about a bizarre encounter he had at Fort Dade. The park ranger said he was strolling after dark along the southern section of the fort where the batteries are located when he heard the unmistakable sound of doors slamming. A few minutes later, the figure of a man began walking toward him out of the shadows. The man was wearing the uniform of a Civil War soldier. The phantom soldier stopped four feet away from the ranger and stared at him for about a minute. Then the soldier turned around, walked a few steps, and vanished.

A number of different ghosts may be responsible for the paranormal activity on Egmont Key. The spirits of Spanish and British soldiers could still be vying for control of the key. The ghosts could be the spirits of the Seminole Indians who suffered from hunger and privation during their incarceration on the island. The ghosts of Confederate soldiers who were forced off the island could have returned to take possession of it. The spirits of the soldiers who manned Fort Dade could be reluctant to relinquish their posts. The lighthouse keepers who, along with their families, called Egmont Key home could have returned to their posts out of a sense of duty to the mariners who depended on them.

Chapter Six

Fort Myers

The Esperanza Pullman Car

In 1971 the railroad tracks and warehouse on Peck and Monroe Streets were sold to the city of Fort Myers. A library was constructed next door to the old train depot, but the depot itself sat vacant until 1975, when a group of citizens raised $400,000 to help foot the cost of transforming the old building into a museum. The city agreed to defray the remaining costs. On April 2, the Southwest Florida Museum of History became a reality. The museum's exhibits trace the history of southwest Florida, beginning with the Calusa Indians and leading up to the impact of World War II. Some of these exhibits include a 1926 La France fire pump, a replica of a pioneer Cracker house, and a 1929 Pullman car that may be carrying some spectral passengers.

The Esperanza Pullman car, which is the longest train car ever built by the Pullman Company, was custom designed for Harry Black in 1929. The luxury car had eight staterooms, each with its own toilet. Three tons of ice stored in the roof provided guests with a primitive form of air conditioning. The walls in the hallway were lined with Cuban mahogany. Servants were summoned by means of several bells located throughout the car.

In 1985 the Esperanza Pullman car was donated to the City of Fort Myers. Almost immediately, visitors and staff members began passing around stories about ghosts. In 2005 the Peace River Ghost Trackers conducted a paranormal investigation of the old train car. By the end, several of the members had had some startling experiences. One person detected a syrupy smell in the lobby, and someone else described the same odor as sweet and cigarlike. Several people encountered a foul smell in the kitchen and dining room and noticed that the smell seemed to follow them into other parts of the train car. One night an investigator was setting up his equipment alone when a three-legged table was thrown at him. An investigator noticed an impression on a bunk in one of the staterooms; it appeared that someone had been lying there. A camera that had been set up in the kitchen made a strange clicking sound, and the investigator who had set up the camera reported that it had been moved after he left the room.

The Southwest Florida Museum offers a number of tours throughout the year, including a museum tour, a downtown walking tour, and escorted day trips to Florida's cultural and historic sites. From a ghost hunter's perspective, the most fascinating tour is the Esperanza Pullman car.

The Burroughs House

One of the most beautiful sites in downtown Fort Myers is undoubtedly the Burroughs Homes and Gardens at 2505 1st Street. In 1899 a Montana cattleman named John T. Murphy fell in love with Fort Myers during a business trip and decided to make it his permanent home. He bought 450 feet of waterfront property and hired an architect from Knoxville, Tennessee, named George Bar to design his dream home. When construction of Murphy's two-and-a half-story, 6,000-square-foot home was completed in 1901, it was the first of a number of luxury homes that would grace the part of 1st Street that came to be known as Millionaire's Row. Murphy's personal touches included stained-glass windows, balustrades, a widow's walk, and a broad veranda. Unlike most homes of this time, Murphy's mansion had indoor plumbing, electricity, and an intercom system through which the Murphys called servants. On the second floor were four bedrooms and a large landing. The servants' quarters were located on the third floor. On the grounds, the Murphys created an exotic garden consisting of ficus, bougainvillea, a gazebo, and a grotto.

In 1918 Nelson and Adeline Burroughs moved into the home. Nelson, a transplanted Yankee from Chicago, ingratiated himself with Fort Myers' growing business community. He and Adeline had four children during their sixty-year marriage. Their two boys, Roy and Raynor, died tragically. Their serious-minded daughter, Jettie, managed her parents' business affairs. The younger daughter, Mona, was a free spirit who married four times. When they were not tending to their children, Nelson and Adeline traveled the world.

Mona was the last member of the Burroughs family to live in the house. When she died in 1978, she willed her home to the City of Fort Myers so that it could be used as a library or museum. In 1984 the Burroughs Home and Gardens was listed on the National Register of Historic Places, and it was designated a local historic landmark in 1994. Today the Burroughs Home is managed by the Uncommon Friends Foundation. It is a popular setting for weddings, receptions, and special events. It is also, some believe, a repository for several ghosts.

In 1993 a reporter for the *Fort Myers Observer* named Wayne Carter sought permission to bring psychic Ruth McGrath to the Burroughs Home and Gardens. His request was denied, so he and his sister, Patti Burns, positioned Ruth on public property in front of the mansion. Her psychic impression of the house was that several spirits inhabited it: a tea drinker, a melancholy man, a bride in a long white dress, and several individuals who longed to leave. Both Ruth and Patti reported feeling pain in their solar plexus, as if they had been punched or shot. Carter later wrote an article about the psychic's revelations.

The staff at the Burroughs Home and Gardens now appreciate the benefits that a haunted reputation can bring to a historic home. Since 2010 the Uncommon Friends Foundation has held its Spirits on the Gulf event, which features ghost stories about the Burroughs Home and other haunted sites in Fort Myers. Some of the stories are told by volunteers dressed as historical figures like Mona Burroughs. During the fundraiser, guests can savor fine wine and dishes prepared by several local restaurants.

Chapter Seven

Gasparilla Island

The Ghost of José Gaspar

Gasparilla Island was named after a famous Florida pirate named José Gaspar. As legend has it, he was born in Spain in 1756 and enlisted in the Spanish navy as a boy. In 1782 his theft of the Spanish crown jewels was discovered. He avoided arrest by commandeering a ship to the Gulf of Mexico. In order to escape undetected, however, Gaspar had to leave his wife and children behind. Gaspar and a group of criminals sailed to present-day Gasparilla, which means "Gaspar the outlaw." Between 1783 and 1821, Gaspar's pirates became the terror of the Gulf Coast. They claimed many ships as prizes. As a rule, Gaspar and his crew killed male passengers. Beautiful female passengers became the pirates' personal playthings or, if they came from wealthy families, were held captive on an island called Captiva. The women were released when their loved ones paid their ransom, which the pirates buried on islands along Florida's southwest coast.

Legend has it that one of Gaspar's abductees was Josefa de Mayorga, the daughter of a Spanish viceroy. She was captured along with her ship, en route from Mexico to Spain and loaded with treasure. Gaspar instantly fell in love with the girl and wooed her with gifts of gold, but she rejected his advances. His crew noticed that he had become morbidly depressed and pleaded with him to execute her. Convinced that Josefa would never love him, Gaspar eventually had her beheaded, but her memory continued to haunt him for years afterward.

In 1822 the sixty-five-year-old pirate was looking forward to retirement. He was planning to share his ill-gotten gains, estimated at $30 million, with his crew. When a ship flying an English flag appeared on the horizon, however, Gaspar decided to claim one more prize. When the ship was within firing distance, Gaspar realized too late that his prey was actually the heavily armed U.S.S. *Enterprise,* which immediately began firing its cannons at the pirates. When it became apparent that the battle was lost, Gaspar wrapped himself in an anchor chain and jumped overboard. The remainder of the pirate crew were hanged from the yardarms or taken to New Orleans, where they were executed.

This is not the end of the story of José Gaspar, however. Local fishermen say that he has never really left the island that he used as his headquarters. Sometimes, late at night, Gaspar's pirate ship can be seen in the waters just off Gasparilla Island, searching for more Spanish merchant ships.

The Old Port Boca Lighthouse

Gasparilla Island is a small strip of land off the east coast of Florida, just north of present-day Fort Myers. In the 1880s, phosphate was discovered several miles just north of Port Boca Grande. The newly mined phosphate was transported on barges to Boca Grande and loaded onto ocean-bound ships. Because the port was now an important stopping-off point for commercial vessels, Congress allocated $35,000 to build a new lighthouse at the end of Gasparilla Island. In 1888 the lighthouse keeper and his family lived inside the lighthouse;

the assistant lighthouse keeper resided in an identical building next door. As a rule, the lighthouse keeper operated the light from dusk until midnight; his assistant worked the light for the rest of the night. The installation was fully manned by lighthouse keepers and their families between 1890 and 1951. Old Port Boca Grande Lighthouse was automated in 1956. Because years of neglect and the effect of the ocean had taken a heavy toll on the building, the U.S. Coast Guard decided to remove the Fresnel lens from the lantern room 1966. Six years later, Lee County acquired the lighthouse and the surrounding thirteen acres. After the abandoned lighthouse was placed on the National Register of Historic Places, the Gasparilla Conservation and Improvement Association contributed $50,000 to the restoration of the old landmark; an additional $50,000 was donated by the Florida Department of Natural Resources. The massive undertaking was completed on November 21, 1986, when the U.S. Coast Guard returned the original light to its rightful place in the lantern room, thereby returning the lighthouse to active service. A citizens group called the Barrier Island Parks Society renovated the lighthouse keeper's house and opened a museum on the site. Today, history and ghost legends live side by side on Gasparilla Island.

A female specter is said to haunt the Old Port Boca Grande Lighthouse. She is the spirit of the young daughter of one of the lighthouse keepers. Legend has it that she succumbed to either whooping cough or diphtheria. For years, tour guides have heard the sound of a little girl playing in one of the rooms on the upper floor, especially at midnight. The little ghost seems to be particularly fond of a doorway in one of the upper rooms.

Except for the fact that the assistant lighthouse keeper's house is now the park ranger's home, the Old Port Boca

Grande Lighthouse looks today much as it did at the turn of the century, thanks in large part to the attention paid to historical detail during the restoration process. Indeed, the authentic appearance of the nineteenth-century building might explain why the spirit of the lighthouse keeper's daughter is reluctant to leave.

As for the ghost of the Spanish girl in the previous story, she seems to be trying to take care of unfinished business, like the other decapitated spirits who stumble through the myths and legends of the American South.

Chapter Eight

John's Pass

The Ghost of John Levique

John's Pass in Madeira Beach is named after the pirate John Levique, whose life has become the stuff of legend. He was a French peasant hired as a cabin boy aboard a Spanish ship that he didn't realize was a pirate ship. The story goes that after the ship had set sail, Levique was given the choice of becoming a pirate or a corpse. He wisely chose the life of a pirate over death. He adapted so well to the pirate life, in fact, that he was given his own ship. However, Levique had an aversion to killing people and consequently didn't acquire much ransom for the people he captured, much to the chagrin of his crew. Somehow, though, he accumulated a chest of gold, which he buried on an island on the west coast of Florida.

After burying his gold, John Levique retired from piracy and became a turtle farmer. In 1848 he and his partner, Joseph Silva, traveled to New Orleans, where they sold a load of turtles. After spending their hard-earned money on wine and women in the French Quarter, the two men returned to Florida to retrieve Levique's treasure chest. The pair were sailing along the west coast of Florida when a terrific storm came up, forcing them to seek safe harbor. After the storm subsided, Levique and Silva made their way to the island where Levique had buried his gold. He was shocked and dismayed to find that the Great Gale of 1848 had cut the island in two, right at the spot where he had buried his treasure chest. The new pass is known today as John's Pass. Levique remained in the area as a turtle farmer until his death in 1873. He never ceased looking for his treasure, however, which he believed had been buried by the sea winds on the beach somewhere.

John's legacy can still be found around John's Pass. Every year, the John Levique Pirate Days celebration features choreographed bar fights and duels, pirate-themed musicals, sea chanties and nautical songs, costume contests, and "real" mermaids at Hubbard's Marina. John Levique's ghost is also a big attraction. In her book *Ghost Stories of St. Petersburg, Clearwater and Pinellas County*, author Deborah Frethem says that many people have seen John Levique's ghost walking along the beach, sometimes during the daylight hours. Witnesses say that he carries a burlap bag in one hand and a long stick in the other. Locals have speculated that he is searching either for turtle eggs or for his long-lost treasure.

Chapter Nine

Key West

Fort East Martello Museum & Gardens

F ort East Martello became obsolete even before it was completed. Construction began during the Civil War era but was halted after the development of explosive shells. Its holdings include historical records, military memorabilia, an eighty-year-old playhouse, the scrap metal "junk" sculpture of Stanley Papio, and the state's largest collection of painted wood carvings and drawings by Mario Sanchez. However, the museum's most popular attractions are its ghosts.

Ghostly soldiers are still at their posts inside Fort East Martello.

Even though no one died in battle at Fort East Martello, the ghosts of former soldiers are still present, apparently unaware that the Civil War ended more than a century ago. Park employees working late at night have heard the scuffing sound of boot soles on the brick walkways in the parade ground. The tunnels in the back wall of the fort are also said to be haunted. When the keeper of the fort first started working there, he was walking his dog through the gates late one evening. The pair had reached the tunnel when the dog's ears stood straight up. His curiosity aroused, the man started walking into the tunnel, but his dog refused to move. The keeper left his dog at the opening and carefully made his way into the tunnel. He was shining his flashlight ahead of him, trying not to trip over the debris that littered the floor, when he made out the image of a man standing about fifty feet from him. The lanky stranger had long, scraggly hair. When the mysterious figure raised his hand in greeting, the keeper thought he was the fort's handyman, but as he approached him, the keeper realized the man was wearing the tattered uniform of a Union soldier. Before the keeper could scream, the ghostly soldier disappeared.

Most of Fort East Martello's activity is caused not by specters but by Robert the doll, who is now on permanent display inside the casement battery. The doll was originally placed inside the alcove. One afternoon, the curator was getting ready to leave her office inside the casement battery. She had stood up and was putting some papers inside her briefcase when she felt someone kick her in the posterior. She turned around and saw a little boy, approximately four years old, run around the corner, giggling. As soon as it dawned on her that the child was wearing a sailor's suit, she ran out of the fort, screaming. The woman did not even return for her bicycle. Robert's temperament greatly improved after he was

Visitors who do not request Robert the doll's permission to take his photograph suffer the consequences.

moved a few feet out of the alcove. Robert now sits in a chair inside a glass case, holding a small stuffed lion. One day, a staff member removed Robert—but not his lion—from the case to clean it. When the man went to retrieve Robert, he was shocked to find the doll holding his toy lion in his hand. One visitor was walking down the hallway after dismissing the notion that Robert is an enchanted doll when a light bulb in a ceiling fan above his head exploded, raining small shards of glass on his head.

Tourists are welcome to take Robert's photograph, but they must ask the doll's permission first. Hanging on the wall behind the doll's display case is a collection of letters from people who did not follow the rule and suffered the consequences. The letters are filled with stories of missed job opportunities, serious accidents, and failed marriages. Robert, it seems, is not a doll to be trifled with.

The Artist House

The beautiful Colonial Queen Anne-style home at 534 Eaton Street was built around 1890. In 1898 the home was purchased by Mr. and Mrs. Thomas Otto, who moved into the house with their three sons. The youngest of the boys, Robert Eugene Otto, inherited the house following the death of his parents. Gene, as he was known to his family and friends, was blessed with artistic sensibilities. He was trained at the Academy of Fine

The Artist House is the former home of Robert the doll.

Arts in Chicago and at the Art Students League in New York. After completing his education in the late 1920s, Gene traveled to Paris, where he met a piano student from Boston named Annette Parker. The couple was married on May 3, 1930. Gene and Anne lived in New York City for a few years while Anne played piano at the Rockefeller Center's Rainbow Room. They then moved back to the family home at 534 Eaton Street, where they lived for the next forty years. Gene passed away in 1974, Anne in 1976.

Today the Otto House is a bed-and-breakfast called the Artist House. Because it is one of the few original buildings in Key West, it has become a regular stop on the Historic Walking Tour and has been featured on ABC Television's *Good Morning America* and Home and Garden Television's *Extreme Homes*. Its architectural and historic significance notwithstanding, the Artist House is of particular interest to fans of the paranormal because it is the original home of Robert the doll.

Robert was created in 1904 by a Bahamian servant for the Ottos who had a deep knowledge of voodoo. Charged with the care of young Gene, the servant discovered that the rumors she had heard about her employers' cruelty were true. One day she became so angry at Mr. and Mrs. Otto that she set about making a special "present" for their son. A few days later, she presented Gene with a three-foot-tall doll stuffed with straw. Gene took an instant liking to the doll and named it Robert. In fact, Gene was so attached to Robert that he carried the doll with him throughout the house. When Mr. and Mrs. Otto overheard their son talking to Robert in his upstairs room, they assumed the doll had become his imaginary playmate. They became concerned, however, when the voice they heard answering Gene was much different from his.

Soon Robert became the talk of the neighborhood.

Neighbors who peered through the windows claimed to have seen the doll walk around the house when the Ottos were gone. Soon Gene's parents began seeing the doll running around corners. Sometimes they thought they heard the doll giggle in Gene's bedroom.

In the weeks that followed Robert's arrival in the Otto household, Gene's feelings of affection for the strange doll rapidly turned to dread. One night Gene's parents were awakened by the sounds of weeping. When they entered their son's bedroom, they were shocked to find it in a shambles. Furniture was overturned, toys were thrown into corners, and clothing was strewn across the room. Gene was sitting up in bed, visibly shaken. With a trembling finger, he pointed to the doll at the foot of his bed and exclaimed, "Robert did it!" This scenario was repeated several times before Mr. and Mrs. Otto were finally convinced that Robert was responsible for the disturbances in the house. Mr. Otto carried the doll up to the attic in the hope that the terror it had instilled in his son would eventually fade. Neighbors, however, kept the stories of the weird doll alive. Many people reported seeing Robert moving around in the attic. Visitors revived the Ottos' memories of Robert with their questions about the footsteps and bizarre laughter emanating from the attic. The Ottos had become immune to the eerie sounds by blocking them out of their minds. Eventually the Otto House became so forbidding that people stopped visiting the Ottos altogether; schoolchildren walked across the street to avoid coming too close to Robert's domain. Gene's last encounter with Robert occurred late one afternoon when he summoned up the courage to enter the attic. There, sitting in a rocking chair, was the doll his father had laid on the attic floor months before. The boy ran down the attic stairs, screaming. When he reached the first floor of the house, he vowed never to enter the attic again.

Robert remained in the attic for many years. By the time Gene Otto died on July 25, 1974, most of the stories of the demonic doll had become a distant memory. The doll's sinister past was revived two years after the death of Anne Otto, however, when a plumber was installing a toilet in the attic for the new owners. According to David L. Sloan, author of *Ghosts of Key West*, the plumber noticed that every time he walked downstairs and returned to the attic, Robert was in a slightly different position. As he was climbing the stairs on his last trip to the attic, the plumber heard childish laughter. When he entered the attic, he was shocked to find that Robert was now on the other side of the room. The plumber was so frightened that he ran down the stairs, leaving his tools in the attic. He never returned.

In the mid 1970s, the Ottos' old house was rented by two men. They too heard the giggling and the patter of little feet running across the attic floor. The first few times the men heard the disturbances, they investigated, fully expecting to find an intruder. Not only did they never find anyone in the attic, but they could tell that Robert had moved a little bit.

At one time, the Artist House was owned by a family who had a ten-year-old daughter. Her father discovered Robert in the attic and presented the doll to his daughter, who eagerly added him to her doll collection. The family had not lived in the house for very long when Robert began tormenting the little girl. One morning, she told her parents that Robert had walked around her bedroom during the night. A few days later, her screams roused her parents from their sleep. As tears welled up in her eyes, she told them that Robert had climbed onto her bed and tried to grab her. When the girl recounted the tale thirty years later, she said she was convinced that Robert had wanted to kill her.

Eventually the passing of time took its toll on the old doll. When Robert was donated to the Fort East Martello Museum & Gardens, he was in pretty bad shape. His little sailor's uniform had yellowed, straw was poking through the fabric on his face, and he was missing an ear. After the doll was repaired, he was placed in a glass case, where he remains to this day.

After Robert was moved to East Fort Martello, many locals expected that the old house would "settle down" and become a typical Victorian home. Robert might be gone, but he seems to have been replaced in the Artist House by the spirit of a woman, quite possibly Anne Otto. Several years ago, a Discovery Channel program titled *Would You Believe It?* reported that the specter of a beautiful woman wearing a wedding gown has been seen walking down the staircase. My wife, Marilyn, and I may have made Anne's acquaintance when we spent the night in one of the second-story rooms a few years ago. The next morning, Marilyn informed me with a smile on her face that something weird had happened to her the night before: "I was awakened at four A.M. by the sound of a door opening. I had just turned over and tried to go back to sleep. Suddenly the room got really cold. Then I heard footsteps in the room. The next thing I knew, the covers were being jerked and pressed down over my feet, which were sticking out from under the covers. It felt like someone was pulling the covers over my feet and firmly tucking in the covers under the bed. I usually kick the covers off my feet because they get hot. The covers were lifted up and put back over my feet. Then I heard the sound of footsteps. I thought you had done it. I looked over, and you were sound asleep. I don't know what it was, but something definitely covered my feet."

After Marilyn told me her story, I reached for my

glasses on the nightstand. They weren't there so I looked for them all over the room, thinking that I might have placed them somewhere else. After a minute or two, it occurred to me that something paranormal might have been involved in my glasses' disappearance. I looked down at the bench where I had placed my luggage, and there were my glasses, sitting right in front of my carry-on bag. Chills went down my spine when I noticed that my glasses were neatly folded. I never fold my glasses before going to bed.

As we were checking out an hour later, Trevor, the concierge, told me that objects have inexplicably fallen from places and landed on the floor. He then told me about a wedding party that had booked rooms at the Artist House years before: "Two of the girls came downstairs for breakfast in the morning. When they walked into the kitchen, a woman told them that breakfast was no longer being served so they left the house and got breakfast somewhere else. Whey they came back, they found the other members of the wedding party enjoying a great breakfast. The two girls checked to see if the housekeeper or one of the other guests was the lady who had told them there was no breakfast, but they never found her. Their description of the lady matched photographs of Anne Otto."

Trevor went on to say that Anne's ghost had not been seen lately but that she lets the staff know she is still around by interfering with electronic equipment. Trevor had no sooner said this than the computer screen he was staring at went blank. "This has happened before, but not very often," he reported.

The Audubon House

The Audubon House at 250 Whitehead Street was built by ships' carpenters around 1850 for a harbor pilot named Captain John Geiger. By the time he erected his beautiful home, he had built a reputation for himself as a "wrecker" who recovered cargo from ships that had foundered on Key West's hazardous reefs. Geiger received twenty-five percent of the bounty he had salvaged. Between 1835 and 1876, he was involved in fifty-seven court cases dealing with shipwrecks. Many of the lavish furnishings in his house were said to have been salvaged from sunken ships. Some of Geiger's family members speculated that a portion of his riches had been acquired through piracy, although they had no hard proof. Ironically, Captain Geiger was often hired to pilot ships around the same reefs that had made him a wealthy man.

Visitors to the Audubon House have heard footsteps and ⬛⬛⬛ through cold spots in the children's room.

When Geiger died in 1885, he left behind his wife and nine children, a considerable fortune, and the family home. His descendants continued to live in the old house until the 1950s. The house was on the verge of being razed when the Mitchell Wolfson Family Foundation intervened and made the Geiger house the first of Key West's restoration projects. On March 18, 1960, Mitchell Wolfson and his wife dedicated the house as a public museum.

Captain Geiger's house is now known as the Audubon House, named for renowned naturalist John James Audubon, who visited Key West and the Dry Tortugas for nearly two weeks in 1832 to find new birds to add to his Birds of America portfolio. During his stay in Key West, Audubon lived onboard the revenue cutter *Marion* to avoid contracting tropical "night fever," or yellow fever. By the time Audubon left Key West, he had added eighteen new birds to his book, most notably the great blue heron. Audubon was so fond of Key West, some say, that his ghost still wanders around the inlets, looking for birds to use as models for his paintings. Staff members and visitors have seen his spirit wearing a ruffled shirt and long jacket. He is usually standing in the gift shop gallery and on the front porch. He may be admiring his bird prints in the gift shop.

Another apparition has been linked to a nineteenth-century painting of a little girl named Hannah, who died at the age of ten, most likely of yellow fever. The oil painting, which once hung in a hallway in the gallery, was commissioned by the dead girl's parents to remember her. In the early 2000s, the painting was placed in a corner of the children's room. One day the gallery manager claimed to have heard disembodied footsteps walking up the stairs and spectral laughter coming from the room. Visitors to the children's room have also heard footsteps and encountered cold spots. The room was painted a brighter color to make it less "ghost friendly," but the ghostly sightings continued. Some employees believe that the little girl's ghost could be joined by the spirit of one of the Geigers' sons, who died in a fall from an almond tree.

The ghosts of John and Lucretia Geiger feel a strong attachment to the home as well. John's ghost usually appears on the second-story landing, from which he may be gazing out over the ocean, looking for ships that have wrecked on the reefs. His specter has also been seen roaming the grounds, looking for the bounty that he reportedly buried there. Lucretia Geiger's ghost once terrified an employee named Pete as he was opening the Audubon House one morning. According to David L. Sloan, author of *Ghosts of Key West*, Pete had just opened the front door and was moving two chairs onto the porch when he turned around and saw the apparition of a woman around fifty years old standing on the front steps. She

The ghost of wrecker John Geiger has been seen at his beautiful home at 250 Whitehead Street.

was wearing a blue dress, a white apron, and a white cap. She vanished before his eyes.

Another ghost in the Audubon House is Willie Smith, a descendant of John Geiger's. Willie lived on the second floor from the 1940s until his death in 1954. People who knew Willie described him as a shy man who never walked down to the first floor of the house. He was so shy, in fact, that grocery boys put his food in a basket that he pulled up to a second-floor window. Neighbors said that Willie was content living in what can best be described as squalor. Today, whenever docents encounter a bad smell in the house, they say, "Willie, leave me alone. I have to get back to work." Almost instantly, the foul odor vanishes.

The Audubon House is one of the country's best examples of American Classic Revival architecture. Even the lush gardens offer visitors a historic look at 1840s' elegance. The beauty of the house and grounds has made the Audubon House a favorite location for luncheons, dinners, and receptions. Visitors find it hard to leave all of this splendor behind at the end of their stay. Apparently, the home's resident ghosts have the same problem.

Key West Cemetery

Located at the intersection of Margaret and Angela Streets in the northeast section of Old Town is a nineteen-acre burial ground called Key West Cemetery. The cemetery was established in 1847 at the foot of Solares Hill after a hurricane destroyed a beachside cemetery on October 11, 1846. The surge of wind and water was so fierce that hundreds of corpses were washed out of their graves and deposited on the sand dunes of Whitehead Point. No one knows for certain how many bodies are interred at Key West Cemetery. Estimates range from sixty thousand to one hundred thousand graves. Many of the people who found their final resting place at Key West Cemetery were the victims of the Great Fire of 1886, the yellow fever epidemics of 1887 and 1888, and the explosion onboard the battleship *Maine* on February 15, 1898.

This monument to the battleship *Maine* stands inside the Key West Cemetery.

The underground population here includes an eclectic mix, including Cuban cigar makers, soldiers, Bahamian sailors, Protestants, Catholics, Jews, executed criminals, millionaires, and paupers. A number of the grave markers have become the stuff of legend. The epitaph engraved on the headstone of hypochondriac Pearl Roberts reads "I told you I was sick." The epitaph on Gloria M. Russell's gravestone is equally memorable: "I'm just resting my eyes." Several zinc metal markers, called "zinkers," and beautiful angel statues are scattered throughout the old cemetery.

Many people are still buried in Key West Cemetery each year, and paranormal disturbances occur there regularly. Visitors walking through the cemetery just before dusk have claimed to have heard ghostly voices and spectral whispering. The sounds seem to increase in volume as rattled listeners hurry away.

People have also witnessed shadows and apparitions among the tombstones at all times of the day, and some visitors have captured the filmy images of human beings and murky figures. One of the most striking photos depicted a dark, translucent, shadowy form walking through the iron gates. No one saw the spirit with the naked eye. In September 2004, a young man took more than thirty photographs while strolling through Key West Cemetery. When he examined the images on his camera, he was shocked by find the dark silhouette of a child standing behind the wrought-iron fence enclosing a family plot.

The most commonly seen apparition at the Key West Cemetery is the large figure of a Bahamian woman wearing oversized gold hoop earrings and a dark-patterned, wraparound dress. Her prominent facial feature is her glowing white eyes. She seems to be a protective spirit who reproaches anyone foolish enough to desecrate the hallowed burial ground by walking on graves or mocking the dead.

Key West Cemetery's nineteen acres have been divided into sections for Cuban freedom fighters, Confederate Navy sailors, and the men who died on the *Maine*. For the most part, these souls seem to get along peaceably in death. The exceptions are those poor souls who, for reasons beyond our understanding, are unable to find eternal rest.

Marrero Guest House

In 1889 cigar maker Francisco Marrero built the Victorian mansion at 410 Fleming Street to lure the love of his life, Enriquetta, to move to Key West from Cuba. Enriquetta instantly fell in love with the elegant mansion and the man who built it. The couple were married and had eight children. While Enriquetta ran the household, Francisco became one of the

Legend has it that the Marrero Guest House is haunted by the ghost of Francisco Marrero's wife, Enriquetta.

city's most prominent and prosperous cigar makers. Francisco was a devoted family man who left his wife and children only when business called him to Cuba. On one of these trips, he died under mysterious circumstances. Enriquetta's grief over the death of her husband turned to fear when she realized that she now had to raise their eight children by herself.

If Enriquetta thought her life couldn't get any worse, she was wrong. A few weeks after Francisco died, she learned that he had another wife in Cuba. Francisco's first wife, Maria Ignacia Garcia de Marrero, arrived in Key West six months later and engaged Enriquetta in a fierce court battle over who was Francisco's rightful heir. To Enriquetta's dismay, the court decided in Maria's favor. Maria immediately sold the house and Francisco's cigar company and returned to Cuba. Enriquetta and her children were forced to leave their beautiful home. Legend has it that as Enriquetta was being evicted on June 16, 1891, she proclaimed to the small crowd that had gathered outside her former home, "You are witnessing a great injustice today, and though you are removing me from my home, you should know that this house is rightfully mine. With God as my witness, I will always remain here." Enriquetta and all of her children died of tuberculosis or diphtheria within two years of moving out of their home.

Over the next hundred years, Francisco's house passed through a number of different hands, serving as a bordello and a restaurant before becoming an all-male guesthouse in the 1970s. One day two men were on their way downstairs when they saw a woman standing at the foot of the stairs. She was dressed in the fashion of the 1880s. When one of the men told her that ladies were not welcome at the guesthouse, the woman turned around, turned into a fine mist, and vanished.

In 1999 the new owners changed the name to Marrero's

Guest Mansion. Staff and guests soon became convinced that Enriquetta kept her promise to return to her lovely home. In *Ghosts of Key West,* author David L. Sloan recounts that the home's owner was getting the house ready for opening day when he heard typing coming from one of the guest rooms. He couldn't find any typewriters in the house, however. The next day, when he and his son were painting, the lights flickered on and off and the radio changed stations on its own. Not long after Marrero's Guest Mansion opened for business, the owner was awakened late one night by three knocks. When he opened the door, no one was in the hallway.

Since 1999 guests have recorded their paranormal encounters in the guesthouse's ghost log. Several guests have detected the scent of lavender perfume in their rooms. The ghost of Enriquetta appears to dislike negative people. When people who are in a bad mood walk through the main door, the chandelier begins swinging back and forth on its own.

Enriquetta has also been seen in the guesthouse. One night, a woman who had been asleep for two hours awoke when she sensed that someone else was in the room. After she rubbed the sleep out of her eyes, she saw the figure of a woman standing at the foot of her bed. She could see through

The chandelier in the entrance of the Marrero Guest House swings when an unwelcome visitor enters the bed-and-breakfast.

the female figure. The woman tried to wake her husband, but the ghost put its hand over her mouth to keep her quiet. The frightened woman immediately sat up. As soon as her body passed through that of the ghost, it disappeared. Another guest woke up to find a headless, armless, legless torso dressed in a white dress sitting on his arm. When the man tried to wake up his wife with his free hand, the ghost rose from the bed and floated across the room to the bathroom. The couple were relieved to find the bathroom empty.

Written accounts from the guest log indicate that the most haunted room in the Marrero Guest House is Room 18, which was one of the Marrero children's bedroom. The cries of children have been heard inside this room, and the gossamer figure of a female apparition has been seen floating across the doorway connecting Rooms 17 and 18. This particular spirit is seen at night so regularly that some people believe Enriquetta is still checking in on her children while they sleep. One morning, a woman sitting in front of the mirror in Room 17 saw the reflection of a woman combing her long, black hair.

The possibility that the ghost of Enriquetta Marrero still claims the house as her own doesn't really trouble staff members. They feel that she is a kindly spirit who is making sure that her home is being properly cared for. Her return to the home from which she was evicted more than a century ago can be viewed as a kind of cosmic justice.

The Hemingway House

One of Key West's most popular tourist attractions is writer Ernest Hemingway's former home at 907 Whitehead Street. Hemingway lived in this Spanish Colonial-style mansion with his second wife, the former Pauline Pfeiffer, and their two sons, Patrick and Gregory, between 1931 and 1939. The house was built by a marine architect and shipwreck salvager named Asa Tift in 1851. Because the house sits sixteen feet above sea level and its walls are constructed of limestone quarried from the foundation, it has endured the blasts of a number of hurricanes over the years. The first home in Key West to have indoor plumbing, it was wired for electricity in 1899. By the time Hemingway arrived in Key West in 1929 on the advice of his friend, author John Dos Passos, the Tift house had stood abandoned for several years and was in dire need of repair, but he and Pauline realized the old house's potential. In 1931 Pauline's uncle, Gus Pfeiffer, purchased the old house at a tax auction for Pauline and Ernest as a belated wedding present for $8,000.

The Hemingways immediately set about restoring the house. Pauline had a deep-well-fed swimming pool built for Ernest while he was recovering from reporting the Spanish Civil War. When he returned from Spain, he was so appalled

The ghost of Ernest Hemingway has been seen staring out of the bedroom window of the Hemingway House.

at the staggering cost of the first in-ground pool in Key West—$20,000—that he exclaimed, "Well, you might as well have my last cent!" He removed a penny from his pocket and pressed it between the flagstones at the north end of the pool. In 1935 he hired a friend to construct a wall around his house to keep tourists from peering through his windows and walking through the front door. Ernest also built a boxing ring behind the house and invited local boxers to spar with him. The water fountain in the yard is actually an old urinal that Ernest took from Sloppy Joe's Bar.

Pauline and Ernest furnished their stately mansion with antiques they bought in Europe, such as an eighteenth-century Spanish walnut dining table, porcelain sculptures, and paintings. The walls are festooned with the heads and skins of animals Ernest shot in Africa and the American West in the 1930s. Living animals have also become indelibly associated with the Hemingway House. Descendants of a six-toed cat that Ernest is said to have received as a gift from a sea captain still stroll around the grounds.

The friends Hemingway made at Key West during this time, such as hardware store owner Charles Thompson and Captain Eddie "Bra" Saunders, became known locally as the Mob. Hemingway and his friends went on fishing excursions for tuna and marlin in the Dry Tortugas, Bimini, and Cuba for weeks at a time. His buddies gave him the nickname Papa, which stuck with him for the rest of his life. However, Hemingway didn't spend all of his time in Key West drinking and fishing. He spent hours in his second-floor studio, finishing the final draft of *A Farewell to Arms* and writing a number of fine short stories, including "The Short Happy Life of Francis Macomber" and "The Snows of Kilimanjaro."

Pauline and Ernest divorced in 1939, and he moved

to a farm called La Finca de Vigia in Cuba. Pauline continued to live at the house with her sons from 1940 to 1951. After Pauline's death in 1951, the house was maintained by live-in caretaker Toby Bruce. In 1961 Pauline's sons sold the house at a silent auction to the owner of the Beachcomber Jewelry Store, Bernice Dixon, for $80,000. In 1964 she converted the main house into a museum and moved into the rear guest quarters. After Bernice moved to a home in the Lower Keys in 1968, the guest quarters housed the Bookstore. Bernice's family inherited the house in the late 1980s after her death, and they continue to run it as a house museum to this day.

It is fitting that Ernest and Pauline's ghosts still abide as the Key West home where they spent so many pleasurable hours with their children and friends. Ernest's presence has been felt in his second-story studio. The clacking sound of his typewriter occasionally echoes through the house. Hemingway's apparition has been seen on several occasions walking through the house. Neighbors have reported seeing a

Some visitors believe that Ernest Hemingway's spirit is still present in his carriage house studio.

spectral figure that bears a striking resemblance to Hemingway staring out a second-floor window at midnight, and passersby claim to have seen the writer's ghost waving to them from inside the carriage house. Pauline's ghost is also an active presence in the house. Tour guides and tourists have seen her ghost standing on the central staircase, looking out the window, possibly keeping watch for her boys.

In the 1930s, Ernest told his friends on a number of occasions that he wanted to spend the afterlife in his Key West home. Some of the visitors and tour guides at the Ernest Hemingway Home and Museum truly believe that the famed author got his wish.

Old Town Manor (Eaton Lodge)

Old Town Manor on 511 Eaton Street is a bed-and-breakfast that once went by the name Eaton Lodge. Samuel Otis Johnson built the house just a short while after the Great Fire of 1886. Around the turn of the century, the three-story Greek Revival mansion was the home of Dr. William Warren, who was the only surgeon in Key West at the time. When his wife, Genevieve, was not tending to their children, she worked in her beautiful garden. Genevieve was particularly proud of her collection of orchids. The Victorian mansion has been so lovingly restored that it received a Rehabilitation Award from the Historic Florida Keys Foundation and is listed on the National Register of Haunted Places. Locals believe that the extensive remodeling might have awakened the dormant spirits of the former occupants of the old house.

Dr. Warren is said to have performed a large number of procedures inside his house. He appears to be a pensive spirit who roams the hallways, apparently deeply concerned about the patients trusted to his care. Guests have reported hearing footsteps outside their rooms late at night. The person seems to be walking back and forth, as if he is lost in thought. David L. Sloan, author of *Ghosts of Key West*, tells the story of a guest who was awakened by the annoying sound. Just as the walker was about to pass her room, she opened the door and was shocked to find the hallway empty. The woman wasn't surprised to find out the next morning that her room used to be Dr. Warren's office.

Dr. Warren's great-grandson was visiting the lodge one night when he heard the distinctive clacking of an old-fashioned typewriter. Understandably puzzled at first, he then recalled that Dr. Warren used to type out his speeches late at night on a manual typewriter. The few witnesses who have actually seen the doctor's ghost describe him as a man in an old-fashioned suit.

Genevieve Warren's spirit strolls around her garden in a formal gown. She is also credited with disturbing the sleep of a young woman who was staying in Room 6, the most haunted

The ghost of Dr. William Warren has been heard pacing back and forth outside his office in the Old Town Manor.

room in the house. Sensing that she was being watched, the guest woke up and saw the distinct form of a woman in a white gown standing at the foot of her bed. At first she thought the female figure was her roommate. However, when she shone her cell phone on the bed, she saw her roommate, sound asleep. She turned her phone toward the foot of the bed, but the apparition had vanished.

Some of the home's poltergeist-like activity that occurs with some regularity has been attributed to the mischievous ghosts of twin girls who lived in the house in the late 1800s. The playful spirits are said to move small objects to different locations and turn the lights and radios on and off. The little apparitions could be responsible for interfering with the electronic equipment that paranormal investigators have brought to the house.

The ghost of a nurse who worked for Dr. Warren could also be haunting the old house. Some guests have complained that they were awakened by the feeling of icy fingers on their wrists, as if someone was taking their pulse. When they woke up, no one was there.

The night my wife and I stayed at Old Town Manor, the desk clerk told me there was only one time she has felt "weird" since she started working at the bed-and-breakfast. "I was sitting at the desk late one evening by myself. Suddenly the door behind me flew open, and I felt a really cold chill. It was pretty scary."

These days, Old Town Manor is one of the homes featured on the Old Island Restoration Federation Christmas Tour of Historically Significant Homes. Visitors marvel at the antique furnishings in the individually decorated guest rooms. Not surprisingly, the old house is also a regular stop on some of the local ghost tours that expose visitors to the "dark side" of Key West.

The Chelsea House Pool and Gardens

The Chelsea House Pool and Gardens at 709 Truman Avenue was originally the residence of the Delgado family. Built in 1870, the Queen Anne–style mansion was a fitting home for one of the largest manufacturers of cigars in Key West. To all appearances, the Delgados were a loving, upper-class family of good standing in the neighborhood. People began to suspect that their marriage was in trouble one October day, however, when Mrs. Delgado informed her loved ones that her husband had returned to Cuba and probably wouldn't be coming back to Key West. The gossips in Key West assumed that the cigar baron had fled to Cuba with his mistress. Most people, especially women, sympathized with Mrs. Delgado, whom they saw as the abandoned wife of an unfaithful husband. These same people were understandable shocked and dismayed

Guests have reported smelling the pungent aroma of cigar smoke inside the Chelsea House.

when Mrs. Delgado, lying on her deathbed in the early 1900s, confessed that she had murdered her husband and buried his body underneath the house, but she didn't reveal the exact location. After she died, the authorities searched under the house and dug under the porch but were unable to find any trace of a corpse. By the time the Delgado Mansion had been converted into a fashionable bed-and-breakfast called the Red Rooster Inn, the old wooden porch had been replaced by a set of stone stairs and landing. It had also gained the reputation of being haunted.

Reports of paranormal activity in the old mansion began surfacing in the 1950s when a couple were awakened by the spectral figure of a man in nineteenth-century clothing who appeared to be lost. The ghostly image faded without interacting with the terrified guests. People also reported the sweet smell of cigar smoke in places where no one had been smoking. In many haunted places, strange smells portend a ghost's appearance. This certainly seems to be the case with the cigar-loving spirit of Mr. Delgado. In his book *Ghosts of Key West*, author David L. Sloan tells the story of a couple who were having difficulty falling asleep because of the unmistakable odor of cigar smoke. While the husband walked out to the pool at the back of the house, his wife slowly drifted off to sleep. She awoke when she felt someone sit down next to her on the bed but was shocked to find that the person wasn't her husband. Her piercing scream brought her husband back to the room. His wife pointed a trembling figure at the bed and insisted that a man had been sitting there when she woke up, but no one was there. She calmed down only after her husband convinced her that she had been having a bad dream.

According to staff at the Chelsea House Pool and Gardens, most of Mr. Delgado's manifestations seem to be confined to Room 18, usually during October, the same month he went missing. Paranormal investigators have taken unusually high EMF readings around the dresser, bathroom, and television. A guest staying in Room 18 was annoyed that the television flickered when she tried to watch it but was fine when her mother began watching.

Most witnesses say that Delgado's ghost looked right through them as if they weren't there. Paranormal investigators describe Mr. Delgado's ghost as a residual spirit who can never leave the place where his life was taken from him so abruptly. Perhaps if his remains are ever discovered, Mr. Delgado will find peace at last.

The Hard Rock Café

Key West's Hard Rock Café is located in a large house at 313 Duval Street. William Curry, the city's first millionaire, built the house for his son, Robert, as a wedding gift. However,

Robert Curry, the son of Key West's first millionaire, killed himself in a bathroom in what is now the Hard Rock Café.

neither the elegant mansion nor the money the sickly young man inherited guaranteed him a happy life. After making several poor business decisions, Robert eventually lost all of his money. One day, he climbed the stairs to the second floor, walked into the bathroom, and shot himself. According to customers and servers at the Hard Rock Café, the despondent spirit of Robert Curry still goes about his daily activities, totally oblivious to the fact that his house is now a restaurant.

Robert's ghost has been described by customers and employees as a dark-haired man who roams the hallways and then vanishes. One of the managers of the Hard Rock Café named Mike said he was closing down the bar late one night when he saw a strange man walk across the room. Before Mike could say anything, the ghostly figure slowly faded.

Robert Curry's spirit has manifested in other ways as well. Brian, a server at the restaurant, says that several years ago, he and one of the other servers were sitting outside, taking a break. Brian happened to look up at a second-floor window

The chandelier in the Beatles Room in the Hard Rock Café has been known to swing on its own.

and noticed that the chandelier was swinging in the Beatles Room. "I raced up the stairs. As soon as I reached the doorway of the Beatles Room, the chandelier stopped swaying." Brian remembered that Robert Curry shot himself in the bathroom in the Beatles Room. He also recalled getting the chills on a couple of occasions when he walked into the Beatles Room.

Robert's ghost also makes its presence known inside the women's bathroom. "We had a hostess named Andrea," Brian said. "She was upstairs in the ladies' room in one of the stalls. Suddenly the handle started jiggling violently, and the door to the stall burst open. She screamed and ran out of the building."

The door to the upstairs bathroom where Robert committed suicide opens to a large piece of plywood. The fact that the scene of Robert's death is inaccessible hasn't deterred people fascinated by the paranormal from visiting the restaurant. Ghost hunters place the Hard Rock Café high on their lists of must-see haunted places in Key West.

Crowne Plaza La Concha Hotel

Carl Aubuchon was an entrepreneur who envisioned a luxury hotel that would accommodate everyone coming to Key West on a train. Construction began in 1925. The seven-story hotel was completed almost a year later at a cost of $760,000, and Aubuchon spent an additional $130,000 on furnishings. On January 22, 1926, the La Concha Hotel opened its doors. Guests were entranced by the artistically designed furniture and the hot and cold running water in the bathrooms, a novelty at the time. In the 1920s and 1930s, the luxury hotel was popular with visiting celebrities. Not only did presidents and foreign dignities spend the night there, but so did artists and writers. Ernest Hemingway worked on his novel *To Have and Have Not* at the La Concha, and Tennessee Williams finished writing *A Streetcar Named Desire* there.

The La Concha Hotel's fortunes dwindled drastically following the stock market crash of 1929. In 1930 the new owners changed the hotel's name to Key West Colonial, but it still lost money, despite the fact that construction of the Overseas Highway was bringing in more visitors to Key West. Five years later, the Labor Day Hurricane destroyed sections of the new highway, thereby isolating Key West from the rest of the state. The La Concha Hotel's deterioration began during World War II and continued up until the early 1980s, when only the kitchen and the rooftop bar were open to the general public. The old hotel was rescued by architect Richard Rauh, who used period photographs to rejuvenate the La Concha. When it reopened its doors in 1986, the La Concha sported a new coral-pink exterior. The past lives on in the tales of guests who never checked out.

Any building that has been the site of multiple suicides is bound to gain a haunted reputation, and the La Concha Hotel is no exception. Thirteen people have jumped to their death from the observation deck, including a

The spirits of people who have jumped from its roof still haunt the La Concha Hotel.

lawyer who was facing disbarment. His despondent spirit has been seen walking back and forth on the observation deck, contemplating the big leap. The spirit of a man who took his own life after drinking a glass of Chardonnay is credited with knocking glasses of Chardonnay out of the hands of patrons at the bar.

The La Concha Hotel is also haunted by the ghost of a man who died accidentally. Shortly after the restored La Concha Hotel opened its doors, a waiter who had just finished cleaning up after a New Year's Eve party on the fifth floor pushed his cart laden with dirty glasses, plates, and silverware to the elevator. When the elevator door opened, he backed his way inside, not realizing that the elevator car hadn't arrived yet. The unfortunate waiter plummeted five stories to his death. His restless spirit is said to wander the fifth floor, occasionally startling guests by tapping them on the shoulder. Guests and

The ghost of Ernest Hemingway is said to be responsible for the paranormal activity in the Hemingway Suite at the La Concha Hotel.

employees have also reported hearing a bloodcurdling scream followed a few seconds later by a loud crash near the elevator on the fifth floor.

The most haunted room in the La Concha Hotel is the Hemingway Suite. Two guests staying in the suite at different times asked to be moved to a different room because of the "weird things" happening there. They complained that the television turned on by itself and that they felt as if someone was sitting next to them on the bed.

The La Concha Hotel stands as a link between the past and the present. Guests can immerse themselves in the old hotel's 1920s' ambience while taking advantage of such modern conveniences as high-speed Internet access and the fitness center. The occasional appearance of the hotel's ghosts reminds visitors that the past is never far away at the La Concha Hotel.

St. Paul's Episcopal Church's Cemetery

The City Council of Key West formally established St. Paul's Episcopal Church at a public meeting in 1831. In 1832 the widow of John William Charles Fleming donated the land for the church site on the condition that her husband's grave remain on the property. The original church, which was built of coral rock, was completed in 1839 at a cost of $6,500, but a hurricane destroyed the building on October 11, 1846. Construction of a second church was completed in 1848. The bishop of South Carolina, Right Reverend C.E. Gadsen, consecrated the church on January 4, 1851. The rectory was built on the corner of Duval and Eaton Streets in 1857. The Great Fire of 1886 destroyed the second church but spared the rectory. A third church was built on the center of the block facing Eaton Street in 1887, but it was destroyed by a hurricane on October 11, 1909. Two years later, the board finalized plans for the construction of a new concrete church on the corner of Duval and Eaton Streets. On June 8, 1919, the first services were held at the church's present location at 401 Duval Street. Because the concrete had been mixed with sea water, the steel reinforcing within the walls expanded and rusted, making the building unstable. The $1-million restoration of the old church began in 1991 and was completed in 1993.

As fascinating as the history of St. Paul's Episcopal Church is, it is the cemetery behind the church that attracts the attention of ghost hunters. Although none of the ghosts haunting the cemetery have been positively identified, folklorists believe that John William Charles Fleming's spirit is probably the apparition dressed in nineteenth-century clothing who makes an occasional appearance in the cemetery. Because his grave behind the church has no marker, the location of his

According to legend, John William Charles Fleming is buried beneath St. Paul's Episcopal Church.

Ghostly children are said to hover near the statue of an angel behind St. Paul's Episcopal Church.

final resting place has never been positively identified. Some locals have even speculated that Fleming's corpse might be under the church itself.

Spectral children have been seen sitting around the statue of an angel in a corner of the cemetery. Another group of children haunt a different part of the cemetery and may be the ghosts of children who perished in a nearby fire. The belligerent spirit of a man who drove pirates out of Key West has been said to attack visitors to the cemetery. A few tourists have reported being frightened by a ghostly sea captain.

Cemeteries have always been ideal places to capture paranormal activity, and St. Paul's Church's cemetery doesn't disappoint ghost hunters. Many of the photographs taken in the cemetery contain orbs and mists that were not visible to the naked eye, especially around the graveyard garden. St. Paul's, it seems, is the church home for both the living and the dead.

Captain Tony's Saloon

The old building that is now home to Captain Tony's Saloon was not always a fun place to hang out. When it was first built at 428 Greene Street, it served as both an icehouse and the city morgue. A wireless station operated from the building in the 1890s. In 1898 the news that the battleship *Maine* had exploded was broadcast all over the world from this building, which later became a cigar factory and a bordello. In the 1920s, several speakeasies set up business here, the most famous of which was the Blind Pig. In the 1930s, Joe "Josie" Russell opened Sloppy Joe's Bar. His most famous customer was Ernest Hemingway, who spent his evenings here between 1933 and 1937. When Russell's landlord raised the rent by one dollar per week in 1938, Russell and his most loyal patrons picked up the barstools, tables, chairs, and all of the other furnishings and carried them over to 201 Duval Street. Hemingway took one of the bar's urinals to his house, where it remains to this day. In 1940 Morgan Bird opened up a gay bar in the former Sloppy Joe's. It did a good business until the U.S. Navy declared the bar off-limits to sailors. In 1958 a local charter boat captain named Tony Tarracino bought the bar and christened it Captain Tony's Saloon. Jimmy Buffet, who performed there in the 1970s, wrote a song about Captain Tony's called "Last Mango in Paris." Tony sold the bar in 1989 but made guest appearances every Thursday until his death in 2008. Captain Tony's became popular with locals and tourists alike. The barstools bear the names of famous people who have had a drink there, such as Bob Dylan and Tennessee Williams.

In recent years, Captain Tony's has attracted the attention of another demographic: ghost hunters. Captain Tony's is said to be haunted by the ghost of a woman named

Captain Tony's Saloon has served as a radio station, an icehouse, a morgue, and Ernest Hemingway's favorite watering hole.

The "blue lady" is the ghost of Elvira Edmunds, who was hanged from this tree inside Captain Tony's Saloon.

Elvira Edmond, who killed her husband and was hanged from the tree that grows inside the bar. The female apparition is called the Blue Lady because she was wearing a blue nightgown on the day she was hanged. Captain Tony made the Blue Lady's acquaintance shortly after he and his girlfriend moved into their room on the second floor. For three nights in a row, he heard the front door open in the middle of the night. On the fourth night, he walked downstairs and crouched behind the tree. In a few minutes, he saw the lady in blue walk through the front gate toward the tree. Then she walked through the tree and through him as well. Over the years, witnesses have said that she floated across the barroom floor and then disappeared into the wall.

Apparently, the Blue Lady enjoys locking the doors of occupied stalls in the ladies' room. Many women have refused to stay long in the ladies' room because they sense that something or someone doesn't want them there. One afternoon, a woman stopped in the bar and asked permission to take her son to the bathroom. The men's room was locked so she told him to use the ladies' room. A few minutes later, the child came running out of the room, claiming that scary voices were saying "bad words" to him. Women who are putting on their makeup claim to have seen the reflection of the Blue Lady in the mirror with her mouth open, as if she is trying to say something. The pool room is also said to be haunted. In the early 1900s, this room was a separate building that served as an icehouse and a morgue. Cadavers that ended up in front of the morgue after a hurricane were supposedly buried where the pool table now stands. Captain Tony filled bottles with holy water and embedded them in the walls of the pool room to keep the spirits quiet, but some customers believe it didn't work. Billiard balls have been reported to move around the pool table on their own. Even the ghosts, it seems, enjoy whooping it up at Captain Tony's Saloon.

Fort Zachary Taylor

Construction of Fort Zachary Taylor began in 1845. After Florida became a state five years later, the still-unfinished fort was named after President Zachary Taylor, who had died in office a few months earlier. The three-story fort was not completed until 1860 because of hurricanes, yellow fever, and a shortage of men and supplies. In January 1861, Captain John Milton Brannan received word that he and the forty-four men under his command were to move into the fort and hold it. Fort Zachary Taylor remained in Union hands throughout the entire war. Its primary function was to serve as headquarters for the U.S. Navy's East Gulf Coast Blockade Squadron, which prevented Confederate supply ships from reaching ports on the Gulf Coast. The fort's ten-inch Rodman and Columbiad cannons, with their three-mile range, discouraged the Confederate Navy from even trying to take Key West. Even though the fort wasn't involved in any major battles, its mere presence may have shortened the war by warding off Confederate blockade runners.

A number of significant changes were made in Fort Zachary Taylor after the Civil War. A desalination plant produced drinkable water for the defenders of the fort. Armaments included 140 guns and an ample supple of ammunition. During the upgrades of the 1880s, most of the cannons were buried in the casements to strengthen the fort. To make room for more artillery, the second and third floors were demolished in 1889. Two more batteries, Osceola and Adair, were then added.

Fort Zachary Taylor was activated again during the Spanish-American War. During World War II, most of its nineteenth-century cannons were replaced with antiaircraft turrets and radar equipment. The fort was deactivated in 1947 and turned over to the Navy, which used it to store scrap. In 1971 it was placed on the National Register of Historic Places and in 1973 was named a National Historic Landmark. In 1976 the state of Florida acquired the old fort and turned it into a museum. A moat was dug around the fort to give visitors an idea of what it looked like during the Civil War.

The large number of ghostly sightings over the years suggests that many of the fort's soldiers are still on duty. Death was a fact of life at Fort Zachary Taylor, not from enemy fire but from disease. Yellow fever claimed up to fifteen people a day there in the second half of the nineteenth century. According to legend, some of these people were buried on the parade grounds, which might account for the sightings of ghostly soldiers standing in formation there.

In his book *Haunted Key West*, author David L. Sloan tells the story of a young woman who had just entered a room west of the parade grounds when she heard a raspy voice

A spectral soldier revealed the location of a cannon buried inside Fort Zachary Taylor.

demand, "Give me some water!" The ghost of a little girl makes an occasional appearance at the hospital. Witnesses say she has severe burns on her arms. The most startling residual haunting harkens back to the days when men were hanged from a gallows set up in the middle of the fort. Visitors walking around the fort at noon have claimed to hear the sound of a trap door falling open.

Fort Zachary Taylor's best-known ghost story took place in 1968. Howard England, an architect for the Naval Air Station, had been digging around the old dumpsite for artifacts. One day he was taking a break inside Room 13 when he heard a voice say, "What be you looking for, sonny?" England looked up and saw a man wearing a blue uniform and a white beard standing in front of him. The man introduced himself as Wendell Gardner. England replied that he was looking for the old cannons that had been buried before the Spanish-American War. The soldier's eyes brightened, and he said, "Well, it's here. That's old Betsy. That's my gun. This was my room." After the strange figure faded away, England began digging in Room 13 and, sure enough, uncovered his first cannon as well as a number of cannon balls. Inspired by England's discovery, a team of volunteers eventually uncovered the largest collection of Civil War cannons in the nation.

In his book *Ghosts of War*, author Jeff Belanger recounts the weird experiences of employees at Fort Zachary Taylor. In the early 2000s, a park ranger was closing up for the day when he saw a man standing on top of one of the batteries. The ranger ordered the man to come down. After running down the steps, the man, who was dressed in the uniform of a Union soldier, stood directly in front of the park ranger. The two men stared at each other for a few seconds; then the soldier slowly dissipated. In 2005 employee Harry Smid was standing in front of one of the casements, waiting for a group of visitors to walk by late one night during a Halloween event. He noticed a man sitting on a cistern, but when Smid walked over to the man, he disappeared.

The Banyan Resort and Guesthouse

The Banyan Resort and Guesthouse at 323 Whitehead Street comprises six houses, which served as private residences in the mid-1800s. In the early 1980s, the homes' owners agreed to form the resort. The most interesting of the six houses is the Cosgrove House, which was built in 1850 and was owned by several different families until Captain Phillip L. Cosgrove and his wife, Josephine, purchased it for $1,600. Captain Cosgrove gained fame as the captain of the first ship to arrive

on the scene and rescue victims from the battleship *Maine* in Havana Harbor in 1898. He also served in the lighthouse service until 1906. As his family grew, Cosgrove found it necessary to add a second story and an attic. Following

Mrs. Cosgrove planted this banyan tree in front of the Banyan Resort.

The ghost of Captain Phillip L. Cosgrove walks the halls of the Banyan Resort.

Cosgrove's death, his son, Phillip L. Cosgrove Jr., inherited the house. Thousands of visitors stop by to photograph the huge banyan tree in the front yard, which his wife, Myrtle, planted in the early 1900s from cuttings her husband brought back from the Caribbean. Banyan trees are characterized by their aerial prop roots, which grow above ground, drop down toward the ground, and eventually become indistinguishable from the main trunk. Because banyan trees tend to grow laterally, the Cosgroves' banyan trees have taken up much of the property.

Cosgrove Jr.'s sister, Emma R. Arnold, became the next owner of the old house. The last member of the Cosgrove family to own the house was his granddaughter, who lived there until 1947. When Mr. and Mrs. William Gamble bought the house, they opened it up for tours so everyone could enjoy the home's nineteenth-century splendor.

Two ghosts are said to haunt the Cosgrove House. Captain Cosgrove's ghost has been seen inside the house, and his ghostly footsteps occasionally resound throughout the home. In addition, the ghost of a little girl seems to have a sweet tooth. Guests who have left chocolate candy bars by their bed at night have awakened to find nothing but empty wrappers the next morning. She also eats the chocolates the maids leave on guests' pillows after they have finished cleaning

The Harry S. Truman Little White House

The Truman Annex neighborhood in Old Town, just off Whitehead Street, is composed mostly of condominiums. However, around the turn of the twentieth century, this area was the U.S. Navy Yard. In 1890 a large, white frame building was constructed near the waterfront. This building originally housed the officers' quarters. Quarters A was reserved for the base commandant, and Quarters B was used by the paymaster. The entire building was converted into the base commandant's private dwelling in 1911. Some famous people have stayed there over the years. President Grover Cleveland stayed there in 1912 on his way to the Panama Canal during its construction. During World War I, Thomas Edison lived there while designing forty-one weapons for the U.S. Navy. Between 1948 and 1949, General Dwight Eisenhower held a series of meetings there that led to the creation of the Department of Defense. Between 1955 and 1956, Eisenhower recovered from a heart attack at the officers' quarters. In 1961 President John Kennedy and British Prime Minister Harold MacMillan met in the building to discuss plans for the Bay of Pigs invasion. In 2005 President Bill Clinton and wife Hillary spent a weekend at the former officers' quarters.

However, this building's most famous visitor is

President Harry Truman. In 1946 he was advised by his personal physician to rest up in a warm climate. In November of that year, the exhausted president moved into the home, which had continued to serve as the Naval Station commandant's headquarters throughout World War II. Truman was so taken with the tropical climate and the people of Key West that he returned in 1947 and famously declared his intention to move Congress down to his tropical paradise. Throughout the remainder of his presidency, Truman visited the Little White House every November and December and every February and March. He made a total of eleven visits to his second home, recording each visit in official trip logs.

Despite Truman's abiding love for Key West and the Little White House, no stories of his ghost have ever been reported. However, two other ghosts have made rather dramatic returns to Truman's second home. One day in the late 1940s, Truman was standing in the parlor, playing Thomas Edison's original recording of "Mary Had a Little Lamb" on one of the first phonographs ever made. Truman, two aids, and a security guard were listening to the recording when the front door flew open. As the men stared in amazement, they

The ghost of President Truman's personal maid frightened security guards at Harry Truman's Little White House in the 1980s.

heard footsteps walk into the parlor and stop in front of the phonograph. Suddenly, the lid of the phonograph slammed shut, and the footsteps proceeded out of the parlor.

More ghostly manifestations of a different sort took place decades later. In the 1980s, security guards were hired to patrol the grounds of the Little White House, which had fallen into disrepair. The owner of the security company had a hard time keeping guards on the job because a spectral woman wielding a broom drove them off. After repairs were made in the Little White House, reports of the ghostly woman dwindled to none. Some people believe she was the spirit of Harry Truman's personal maid, Rose, who was angry because the Little White House was allowed to deteriorate.

Even though the building had become Truman's home away from home, it remained the Naval Station commandant's house until 1974, when it was added to the National Register of Historic Places. The old building was vacant until January 1, 1987, when it was transferred to the state of Florida. A fund-raising project started in 1988, and by 1990 Truman's Little White House had been restored to its 1949 appearance at a cost of $1 million. One year later, the house was converted into a state historic site and museum. Today visitors can see the custom-made mahogany poker table where Truman drank whiskey with his cabinet members. They can walk past the bar where Truman added his "engine starter"—a shot of Old Grand-Dad bourbon—to his glass of orange juice each morning. They can gaze at the small wooden table in the living room where Truman signed documents that changed society, such as the executive order to desegregate the armed forces. Chances are good, though, that visitors won't run into Rose's ghost. The absence of sightings since the house was opened as a museum suggests that she is pleased with the restoration of President Truman's beloved home.

88

Chapter Ten

Naples

Cracker Barrel Restaurant

C racker Barrel restaurants have become
synonymous with nostalgia and down-home
cooking. The idea for an old-fashioned type of
restaurant was born in the mind of Dan Evans, whose family
was in the gasoline business. He believed that people were
becoming tired of fast food and were yearning for the slow-
cooked meals of their childhoods. He opened the first Cracker
Barrel in Lebanon, Arkansas, on September 19, 1969. Evans'
idea soon caught on. By 1977 thirteen Cracker Barrels had
opened from Tennessee to Georgia. The company went public
in 1981, and eighty-four stores opened within the next decade.
Today there are more than six hundred Cracker Barrels in
forty-two states. The family-friendly atmosphere that people
associate with Cracker Barrel made the tragedy that occurred
in the Naples store in the mid 1990s particularly shocking.

On November 15, 1995, local police received a frantic
call about a robbery at the Cracker Barrel on 3845 Tollgate
Boulevard just off I-75. The scene that greeted them when they
walked into the store was seared in their memory for years
to come. Three employees—Vicki Smith, Jason Wiggins, and
Dorothy Siddle—were lying on the floor of the freezer in a
pool of blood. Their hands had been tied with electrical tape,

and their throats had been cut. Bloody footprints led through the kitchen to the manager's office, where the police found an open safe and money of different denominations scattered on the floor. Behind the store, police discovered a pair of blood-soaked gloves, an air pistol, a buck knife and knife case, and more money. They also found more bloody footprints leading away from the crime scene.

Thanks to the efforts of police and crime scene investigators, the perpetrators of this heinous crime were apprehended. Two former employees of the Naples Cracker Barrel—Brandy Jennings and Jason Graves—were captured in Las Vegas. At first, Jennings said that he planned the crime but that his partner killed the three employees. Jennings also said that the air pistol belonged to Graves. Later on, Jennings showed police where he and Graves had thrown a Cracker Barrel money bag, packaging for the air gun, shoes, socks, gloves, and a garbage bag. The shoes matched the prints that had been tracked all over the store.

After interrogators brought up the inconsistencies in Jennings' story, he admitted, "I could have been the killer. In my mind, I think I could have killed them, but in my heart, I don't think I could have." Comments Jennings had made to his fellow employees at Cracker Barrel about disliking Siddle were also used against him during his trial. Jennings and Graves were both convicted of three counts of capital first-degree murder and one count of robbery. The prosecuting attorney proved that Jennings had slashed the victims' throats. Graves was convicted of standing guard with the air pistol to keep the victims from escaping. The pair had hoped to make off with $15,000, but they ended up with only a few hundred dollars.

Not surprisingly, the horrific murders that took place on November 15 left a psychic imprint on the walls of Store

#117 in Naples. Lights flicker on and off throughout the store. Employees retrieving items from the freezer have reported having the door close on them. An employee who was cleaning the women's restroom said that one evening the toilets in one of the stalls began flushing repeatedly. On several occasions, employees have discovered packets of sugar and NutraSweet scattered all over the tables when opening the restaurant in the morning. Display items, such as videos, CDs and cookbooks, have been moved to entirely different spots during the night. Many employees have experienced a sense of uneasiness in different parts of the store.

The nightmarish events of November 15, 1995, refuse to fade away into obscurity. Brandy Jennings' failed appeals received media attention for more than a decade. In 2010 he filed a motion for post-conviction relief, claiming ineffective counsel. He and Graves are still on death row.

Chapter Eleven

Ocala

Seven Sisters Inn

The Seven Sisters Inn was originally comprised of two Victorian homes: the pink Scott House, built in 1888, and the purple Rheinhauer House, built around 1890. The Rheinhauer House was built on a battlefield dating back to the Seminole War of 1835. No one knows for certain how many soldiers and Seminole Indians died on the property. In 1886 the house that had stood on the site where the Scott House was built was completely destroyed by fire. Around the turn of the century, Sylvia Scott, one of the seven Scott sisters after whom the inn was named, was trapped in a room on the second floor after a fire broke out. She survived but was emotionally scarred by her brush with death. When the Scott House was transformed into a boardinghouse in the first half of the twentieth century, an elderly lady passed away in a room on the first floor.

In the 1990s, the historic homes were purchased by Bonnie Morehardt and Ken Oden, who converted them into a bed-and-breakfast. The owners of the Seven Sisters Inn had their own encounter with the paranormal not long after moving in, when they heard footsteps in the room right above them on the second floor. They assumed that a guest who was overdue had just arrived so they walked upstairs but were surprised to find the room empty. Bonnie told Jack Powell, the author of *Haunting Sunshine*, that the third floor of the Rheinhauer House was particularly creepy. One day a workman who was making repairs on the old house said he borrowed a hammer from an elderly man. He set the hammer down and left the room and was unable to locate the hammer or the helpful old man later.

After the Seven Sisters Inn was open for business, guests began reporting strange occurrences in their rooms, which are named after famous cities. In the Paris Room, guests returning from a night on the town entered the room to find a man sitting in a chair near a window, smoking a cigar. After a few minutes, the strange man disappeared. An employee said that she too saw the male apparition sitting in a chair. As soon as he disappeared, the chair flew through the air and nearly struck her in the head.

One of the ghosts in the Scott House seems to be a protective spirit. One afternoon, an employee was walking down the staircase when she tripped over something. Just before she lost her footing, something behind her grabbed hold of her shirt and helped her regain her balance. She thanked the ghost for saving her life and proceeded down the stairs.

The Grand Room is the most haunted room in the Scott House. On a number of occasions, guests have taken a book off the mantle. If they didn't place the book back on the mantle exactly the way it was before they disturbed it, the book moved back to its original position while they stood there watching.

The apparition seen most often in the Scott House is probably the spirit of Sylvia Scott. The ghost known as the Lady in White has a phobia of fire, just as Sylvia did after her fiery ordeal. The ghost has been known to blow out candles right after they are lit. Ken Oden said that once he had just lit a stick of incense when he felt an invisible hand grab his elbow. Light bulbs also seem to burn out much faster than they should.

In 2008 the Atlantic Paranormal Society (TAPS)

conducted a formal investigation of the Seven Sisters Inn. While waking around the first floor of the Rheinhauer House, Grant Wilson and Jason Hawes heard someone running across the room right above them. When Grant opened the door to the room, he heard someone whispering. Later when Kris Williams and Dave Tango were on the first floor, they too heard someone running upstairs.

As Jason and Grant were on their way to the India Room in the Rheinhauer House, Jason saw a large shadow person walking alongside them. Using his EMF detector, Grant scanned the India Room. As he passed the EMF detector over a chair, the spikes in the electromagnetic field created the impression of a human body sitting in the chair. When Grant and Jason sat in the chair, they both felt very cold.

Jason's most startling experiences occurred in the Scott House. He was walking up the staircase when he saw the figure of a small child dart out of one of the rooms on the second floor. During the reveal, the owner admitted that he too had seen the ghost of a small child at the top of the stairs. Not long after seeing the child, Jason noticed that one of the flip-flops he had placed on the floor was missing. He looked all over the first floor of the house and finally found it in a closed room that was used for storage. He had no idea how it got there.

In 2010 a pair of attorneys named Richard Perry and Jim Richard purchased the Seven Sisters Inn shortly after a foreclosure action. They converted the Scott House into their law office and hoped to find someone who would lease the Rheinhauer House and run it as a bed-and-breakfast. Except for removing the hot tub on the third floor, they tried to preserve the integrity of the Queen Anne Victorian. They have experienced no paranormal activity, but one wonders if the ghosts will express their displeasure if Perry and Richard go ahead with their plans to change the color of the pink house.

Chapter Twelve

_____

Pass-a-Grille

The Ghost of John Gomez

A ll we know about the life of the self-proclaimed last of the pirates, John Gomez, is his personal account, the credibility of which is suspect. Gomez claimed to have been born in Portugal in 1781. At the age of twelve, he was employed as a cabin boy aboard a ship en route to the United States. Before long, the boy discovered that the ship's captain had a cruel streak so when the ship docked at Charleston, South Carolina, Gomez deserted and made his way to St. Augustine, Florida, where he joined the crew of a merchant vessel. His ship hadn't been out to sea for long before it was captured by the crew of the notorious pirate José Gaspar, Gomez's brother-in-law. Gomez ingratiated himself with the pirates and in 1805 was dispatched to Spain to assassinate one of Gaspar's enemies. However, before he could carry out his mission, Gomez was captured by the French and pressed into service in the French army. He was present when Napoleon Bonaparte marched into Spain. Even though Napoleon himself commended Gomez on his bravery, Gomez deserted the French army and joined the crew of a slave ship. Ironically, Gaspar captured the slave ship, and Gomez once again became a pirate.

He served as a member of Gaspar's crew until the spring of 1822, when the U.S. Navy captured Gaspar's ship. Gomez and the rest of the pirate crew surrendered. Gomez managed to slip away from his captors and joined up with General Zachary Taylor's forces during the Seminole War. On December 25, 1837, Gomez was in the battle of Lake Okeechobee.

In 1857 Gomez arrived in Pass-a-Grille, where he made his living transporting tourists on his boat, Red Jack, to Pass-a-Grille, where he had set up a small resort. His tourist business came to an end in 1861 after Egmont Key fell to Union forces. For a while, he made a living as a blockade runner. Determined to pursue a much less hazardous occupation, Gomez traveled to Panther Island, where he spent the rest of his life fishing. A life-long member of the Roman Catholic Church, Gomez proudly wore a large crucifix around his neck. On July 12, 1900, Gomez drowned when his foot became entangled in the fishing net hanging off his boat. According to the St. Augustine Record, Gomez was 122 years old when he died. Some newspapers gave his age as 118.

Most historians harbor serious doubts about the credibility of Gomez's account, although they agree that he arrived in Pass-a-Grille in 1857. Some people believe that he is still there. His deep voice has been carried along the beach on the spring breezes. He still seems to be telling stories, most of which are probably apocryphal.

Chapter Thirteen

Pensacola

Old Sacred Heart Hospital

For much of Pensacola's early history, people who were sick or injured were treated in local clinics. Serious cases were sent to New Orleans. The Daughters of Charity, a religious order dating back to 1633, rectified this situation by investing $400,000 in the construction of Pensacola Hospital, the first Catholic hospital in Florida. In 1948 the name was changed to Sacred Heart Hospital, which ceased caring for patients in 1965, when the hospital relocated to North Ninth Avenue. Between 1969 and 1978, a private school for liberal arts was housed in the building until maintenance proved to be too costly. The former hospital was purchased by Tower East Group in 1980 and converted into an office building. In 1982 the Old Sacred Heart Hospital became the only hospital in Florida to be added to the National Register of Historic Places. Today a few private offices are located on the lower levels of the building, as well as a number of small businesses such as a yoga studio, a veterinary clinic, and a Montessori school.

The ghost of a nun has been seen on the premises for many years. Until the hospital closed in 1965, nuns claimed to have encountered the kindly ghost as they walked down the hallway to the chapel. A few of them reported feeling someone tap them on the shoulder to get their attention. A young man caught a glimpse of the ghostly nun early one evening in

2012: "We went to the Old Sacred Heart Hospital to get some pizza. It had just rained, and my girlfriend and I were standing outside the car, trying to figure out our order, when I looked up at the top floor and saw a woman in a white robe standing in an open window. I told my girlfriend, and she looked up and saw the same thing. A few seconds later, our friends started getting out of the car. I turned around and told them to look up at the open window. When I looked back, the nun was gone, and the window was closed. We ran inside the building so we could climb the stairs and look for the ghost. When we reached the stairwell, the door was locked." What makes the young man's story even creepier is that the upper floors have been closed to the public for years.

Quayside Art Gallery

The two-story building at 17 East Zarragossa Street was built in 1873 just one block north of the wharves, or quays, where wooden ships once docked. The building was originally used as a firehouse by the Germania Steam Fire Engine and Hose Company. For decades, firemen manning the Maria Louise, a 2.5-ton, horse-drawn, steam-pumping engine, rode furiously through the city, putting out fires. A mural on the side of the building commemorates these unsung heroes. In 1973 a cooperative organization of more than two hundred artists founded Pensacola Artists Incorporated and established an art gallery in the old firehouse. The gallery's mission is to promote the arts in Pensacola by showcasing the works of up-and-coming artists. Thousands of people visit the Quayside Art Gallery each year to gaze at the watercolors, oils, and photographs on display.

Back when the building was used as a firehouse, the firemen lived and slept upstairs. For several nights in 1892, they were awakened by the shaking of the heavy oak doors. When they walked down the stairs and checked on the doors, they found nothing out of order and no trespassers inside the building. A few minutes after the sleep-deprived firemen returned to their beds, they were awakened again by the same weird sounds.

The most terrifying paranormal incidents inside the firehouse were witnessed by firemen Willie Britson and George Suarez, who were sleeping alone in their bunks. They were awakened by the sound of heavy boots stomping around on the floorboards. A few seconds later, they heard furniture being dragged across the floor. The men were lying in their beds, trying to decide whether or not to investigate the noises, when a large blue ball of light began darting across the room. The room suddenly became cold and, to the men's amazement, the orb took the form of a man dressed in white. The strange figure walked from bed to bed and placed its hands on the necks of the firemen. After a few minutes, the apparition vanished. The men were so terror-stricken after the ghost left that they remained in their beds for half an hour, too petrified to leave.

The next day, the two men told their story to a reporter from a local newspaper. When the reporter asked them who they thought the ghost was, the firemen came up with two possible identities. One was a black man named Jeff Lowe who had been hanged in Pensacola a few years before. The other was a fireman who had lost his life in a fire back in the 1880s. After the firemen gave their interview, the sightings dropped off. No one knows why the same specter that was extremely active for a few weeks in 1892 has never returned. Perhaps it accomplished its mission: to make its presence known.

Seville Quarter

The Pensacola Tobacco Company warehouse on Government Street was built in 1871. In the 1930s and 1940s, a brothel was housed on the second floor. Taxi cabs brought in hundreds of sailors from the Naval Air Station to the bordello and picked them up one or two hours later. In 1967 the old building was purchased by Bob Snow, a Dixieland band leader, with the intention of converting one of the largest rooms into a bar called Rosie O'Grady's. Patrons sat on picnic tables and listened to Bob Snow and his band play Dixieland music. Over the next few years, Snow furnished the cavernous building with souvenirs he had purchased on his travels all over the world. In 1988 Snow sold the building to the Mitchell family. Today Seville Quarter, as the building is now called, houses a number of small bars and restaurants, many of which are said to be haunted.

One of the most haunted parts of the building is the second floor, which has been converted into offices. Many people have encountered cold spots inside the ladies' room, and orbs frequently appear in photographs taken in the hallway outside the bathroom. When the Mitchell family was renovating the building, they frequently heard women's voices in the vicinity of the ladies' room. One afternoon, a woman was trying on a Mardi Gras costume inside the bathroom when the temperature dropped. Suddenly, the figure of a young woman floated into the bathroom. The specter had dark eyes and a cream-colored complexion. Her hair was piled on top of her head, and she was wearing clothes from the Victorian period. The apparition stared at the woman for a few seconds before disappearing.

The most famous ghost in Seville Quarter is the spirit of a man known only as Wesley. He was a construction worker in his early forties who was injured while renovating the building for the Mitchell family. He wanted to continue working for the Mitchells so badly that they finally let him mop the floors in Rosie O'Grady's. After a few months, Wesley worked his way up to bartender, a position he had coveted for a long time. One night in 1993, Wesley failed to show up for work. Patrons and employees knew something was wrong because Wesley loved his job and had never been late before. A couple of hours later, an employee walked into the cooler to pick up a case of beer. There, lying on the floor, was Wesley. He was immediately taken to the hospital, where he was declared dead. The exact cause of death is unknown, although most people surmise he had a heart attack.

Wesley's love for Rosie O'Grady's seems to have persisted into the afterlife. He is often blamed for moving glasses around on tables, and he seems to have a strong affinity for electrical appliances, like microwaves, which turn on and

A ghostly employee named Wesley continued showing up for work at this bar in Seville Square in the 1990s.

off for no apparent reason. One night a piano player walked into the piano area, which was completely dark. As he walked up the steps to the piano, the lights came on. Sometimes the piano plays on its own when no one is around.

Wesley also seems to enjoy hanging out in the men's restroom on the first floor. Sometimes when someone is washing his hands, the hand drier comes on by itself. If the person says, "OK, Wesley, I know you're here," the drier turns itself off. Urinals flush themselves, and a number of people have detected the tantalizing fragrance of rose perfume. A few privileged patrons and employees claim to have seen Wesley's ghost in the men's restroom. Witnesses describe him as tall with dark hair, heavy eyebrows, and vacant eye sockets. Some people have felt his presence standing behind them or looking over their shoulder while they standing at the sink.

Another ghost who is very much at home in Seville

Some nights, this piano in Seville Square plays by itself.

Quarter is the spirit of a young employee named Angela, who was murdered in her apartment by her boyfriend in the early 2000s. Like Wesley, Angela loved her job and was well liked by her coworkers. Members of the wait staff who knew Angela sometimes feel a reassuring touch on their shoulder. When they turn around and realize they're alone, they think back to the days when Angela tried to get their attention in the same way.

Some of the other bars and restaurants inside Seville Quarter seem to be haunted as well. One day an employee at Fast Eddie's, a billiards hall, was walking past a pinball machine when it turned on by itself, even though it was unplugged. Late one evening, a couple of employees at the End of the Alley bar were decorating for Halloween when one of them said, "I wonder if Wesley will show up this year." Several glasses hanging from a rack above the bar suddenly flew across the room and smashed against the wall. Women standing at the sink in the bathroom just outside of the End of the Alley bar have heard a voice whispering in their ear. Inside another bar called Phineas T. Fogg's, patrons have seen the ghostly form of a man standing at the bottom of the steps. The beer tap has been known to turn on by itself as well. Employees at a restaurant called Palace Café have opened up in the morning and found the volume of the music turned up high. Inside the restaurant's gift shop, bottles of wine placed on top of a cooler were knocked off by an invisible hand. Not long thereafter, a picture flew off the wall. Most of the time when strange things happen in Seville Quarter, the employees laugh them off as nothing more than Wesley's attempts to get attention.

The Mole Hole

The Mole Hole at 425 East Zarragossa Street is located inside a house built in 1780, one of the oldest surviving wood-frame buildings in the entire city. The Mole Hole is one of those quaint shops that specialize in unique gifts you can't find in larger retail outlets, including a wide selection of hand-blown glass, jewelry, and greeting cards. It is the toys, however, that hold the biggest attraction for children, even those who are no longer among the living.

The Mole Hole appears to be haunted by the spirit of a little boy. He has been seen only by other children, who have described him as wearing knee britches, long stockings, a vest, and a hat. Judging from his clothes, most people assume he died in the house early in the nineteenth century. The little boy is most active during the Christmas season, when a toy Christmas village is put on display. Children enjoy rearranging the figures while their parents walk through the shop. On several occasions, the owner has put all of the figures back in their proper places before closing up, only to find them misplaced again when she opens the shop the next morning.

The Tivoli High House

The Tivoli High House at 205 East Zarragossa Street was built in 1976 on the site of a previous structure that was built in 1805 and demolished in 1937. The ticket office for tours given by the West Florida Historic Preservation Society is housed on the first floor of the "new" Tivoli House, and the offices of the Pensacola Symphony Orchestra are on the second floor. If the stories told about the building are true, not everyone who walks through the front door is of this world.

The original Tivoli High House was built by Jean Baptiste Cazenave, Pedro Bardinave, and Rene Chardiveneau. It was part of a complex that included an octagonal rotunda, the Tivoli dance hall, a kitchen, and a scattering of outbuildings used for gambling and billiards. During one of the city's outbreaks of yellow fever in the late 1830s, a dancer collapsed and began vomiting black blood. The next day, the entire complex was quarantined until the danger of contagion had passed.

In the 1840s, the complex was purchased by Don Francisco Morena, who razed the dance hall to make room for his new home. He then converted the Tivoli High House into the Hotel de Paree. During the Civil War, the Union Army used the hotel as a barracks. After the war, the hotel continued to serve as a boardinghouse until it was torn down in 1937. The Florida American Bicentennial Commission hired local architect Theophalis May to build a reproduction of the Tivoli High House.

Today volunteers dressed in period clothing add an air of authenticity to the Tivoli High House. One summer day, a volunteer was working in the back room when she heard someone walk in the front door. Out of the corner of her eye, she saw a woman moving around the gift shop. Because the woman was wearing an old-fashioned dress, the volunteer assumed she was a volunteer who worked in one of the other historic buildings. When she asked the woman if she could help her, the stranger became agitated. Then she simply faded away. Was the phantom visitor the ghost of a woman who frequented the dance hall or of someone who once lived in the old Tivoli High House?

Old Christ Church

In 1829 the newly formed Protestant Association purchased a lot in Seville Square for $400. Construction of a new church on the site began in 1830 and was completed two years later at a cost of $4,500. Three of the early rectors of the church— Reverend Joseph Saunders (died 1839), Reverend Frederick R. Peake (died 1846), and Reverend David Flower (died 1853)— were buried under the vestry room floor. After most of the church families fled Pensacola in 1861, the Union army used the abandoned building as an infirmary and barracks. They also exhumed the bodies of the three rectors and desecrated them. After the war, the church members who had fled to south and central Alabama returned to Pensacola and repaired the damage to their beloved church. By 1879 the membership had increased so much that the nave of the church was expanded twenty feet to the west. Stained-glass windows were installed in 1884. In 1957 the old church was completely renovated.

In 1988 the fifteenth rector of Old Christ Church, Reverend Betty Madison Currin, invited Dr. Judy Benson from the Archaeological Institute of the University of West Florida to locate the graves of the three rectors. Benson's team located the burial plots of the three rectors underneath the part of the building that had been added in 1879. When they opened the decomposing coffins, they discovered that the corpses had indeed been desecrated.

Boxes containing the bones of the three rectors were taken to the nearby Lear-Rocheblave House, which was being used as a field house for the dig. The archaeology students spent all day identifying the bones and laying them out in individual boxes. The next morning, when the students returned to the Lear-Rocheblave House, they were shocked to find the carefully laid-out bones askew. The boxes looked as if someone had picked them up and shaken them. The old house was securely locked at the time.

A few months later, the bones of the three rectors were reinterred under the floor of the vestry. More than three hundred people gathered to watch the funeral procession as the three coffins were carried down the sidewalk. During the procession, one of the archaeology students noticed something unusual. He saw three men wearing dark robes and scarves around their necks marching in the procession. One of the men held a Bible and stared straight ahead while his two companions carried on an animated conversation. The most striking aspect of their appearance was that all three were barefoot. The young man asked the people standing next to him about the three strange men, but no one else saw them.

Afterward, at the reception, the archaeology student asked Reverend Currin about the three strange figures. She told him that according to tradition, Episcopalian priests are buried barefoot with their stoles wrapped around their necks and a Bible in their hands. The student left the funeral wondering if the three priests had actually participated in their own funeral.

The Dorr House

Ebenezer Dorr was the first territorial sheriff of Escambia County. Ebenezer's son, Eben Walker Dorr, married Clara Barley in 1849. During their twenty-one-year marriage, the couple had five children. After Eben died of yellow fever in 1870, his wife hired a contractor to build a house befitting a woman of her wealth and status. She lived in the Greek

Revival home at 311 South Adams Street until her death in 1896. The house was used as a school for a time and was extensively restored after it was purchased by the Pensacola Heritage Foundation. The Dorr House is now the home of the president of the University of West Florida. It is also a stop on the Historic Pensacola Village tour, one that tends to make tour guides uneasy.

Tour guides have borne witness to a great deal of paranormal activity inside the Dorr House. Guides waiting in the house for a tour to arrive have been overcome by the uneasy feeling that someone is standing just outside of their vision. One guide who was standing at the top of the stairs had just told her group that Mrs. Dorr was "plump" when she felt someone push her from behind. Guides frequently step into the kitchen to demonstrate various kitchen utensils and then resume the tour. The guides later return to the kitchen to put things back in order only to find the utensils already back in their proper places.

Tourists have had strange experiences inside the Dorr House as well. A number of people claim to have seen a woman in a Victorian-era dress sitting in one of the "fainting chairs," probably because her corset was too tight. Visitors passing through the house have felt a disembodied hand tugging on their pants legs. People standing in the sewing room, which was used as the sick room in Clara Dorr's day, have heard the soft sobbing of a woman. Visitors occasionally encounter cold spots and smell the sweet fragrance of roses.

The most commonly seen apparition in the Dorr House is the translucent figure of a woman in her mid thirties, wearing a Victorian-era dress. She is usually standing on the balcony or dancing across one of the upper rooms. As a rule, the specter materializes after an object has been moved to a different location. Her appearance signifies either her pleasure or displeasure at having her possessions relocated.

Fort Pickens

Fort Pickens derives its name from Revolutionary War
hero General Andrew Pickens. The largest of the four forts
defending Pensacola's coast, Fort Pickens was built between
1829 and 1834 under the supervision of Colonel William H.
Chase of the Army Corps of Engineers. More than twenty-
one million bricks went into the building of the fort. Workers
suffered from a variety of ailments, including heat exhaustion
and yellow fever. After the Mexican-American War, Fort
Pickens was unoccupied, but the fort's military significance
increased during the Civil War. In January 1861, Florida
troops under the command of Colonel William H. Chase
demanded that Union Lieutenant Adam J. Slemmer surrender
Fort Pickens. Lieutenant Slemmer's refusal to give up the fort
led to a fierce confrontation on November 22. A two-day
bombardment of the fort ensued, the Confederates retreated,
and Fort Pickens became one of the few forts in the South that
was never under Confederate control.

Phantom voices, groans, and buzzing sounds have been heard inside Fort Pickens.

Over the years, Fort Pickens has undergone a number of drastic changes, including the construction in 1898 of Battery Pensacola, which covers half of the parade grounds. Rifled cannon replaced the old-fashioned, smooth-bore cannon. Fort Pickens received national recognition once again when Apache Indian Chief Geronimo was imprisoned there from October 1886 to May 1887. About twenty people visited the fort each day to catch a glimpse of the famous chief. On June 20, 1899, a fire in Bastion D ignited the one thousand pounds of gunpowder stored in the bastion's magazine. One soldier was killed in the explosion, which completely destroyed Bastion D. Fort Pickens was finally decommissioned in 1947, when it became a state park.

Today Fort Pickens looks so much as it did when it was in active service that it's easy to imagine that its ghostly defenders are still on duty. Indeed, rumors of haunted activity inside the old fort have been circulating since the early 1970s. In his book *Florida's Ghostly Legends and Haunted Folklore*, author Greg Jenkins says that visitors have heard work crews digging on the lawn. Phantom voices bark out orders to unseen soldiers. Groans and buzzing sounds have been recorded inside the fort. People standing in dark corners of the fort have sensed that they are being watched. Shadowy figures are said to patrol the tunnels and rooftops. Fort Pickens may be a relic of Florida's past, but some of the soldiers stationed there years ago haven't gotten the news.

Pensacola Lighthouse

The first Pensacola Lighthouse was built in 1824 by Winslow Lewis. The first lighthouse keeper, Jeremiah Ingraham, married Michaela Penalber in 1826, and the couple raised their three children at the lighthouse. After her husband died in 1840, Michaela assumed control of the lighthouse until her death in 1855. She was succeeded by her son-in-law, Joseph Palmes.

Complaints about the lighthouse in the early 1850s soon led to discussions about replacing it. In 1852 the Lighthouse Board recommended that a new lighthouse be built one half mile west of the original beacon. The floating light vessel *Aurora Borealis* served the port until the lighthouse was finished. Funds to build the second Pensacola Lighthouse were appropriated by Congress in 1856. The tower was 150 feet tall and ranged in diameter from 30 feet at the base to 15 feet at the top. It was outfitted with a first-order Fresnel lens and was first lit on New Year's Day in 1859. After Florida seceded from the Union on January 10, 1861, Confederate troops seized the tower and removed the Fresnel lens. On November 22, 1861, Union troops commenced a two-day artillery battle, during which the lighthouse was struck by a dozen rounds. On May 9, 1862, Confederate forces relinquished control of the lighthouse, and it was taken over by the Union. A fourth-order lens was installed, and the lighthouse was lit once again in December 1861.

Nature launched an assault on the lighthouse in the years following the Civil War. It was struck by lightning in 1874 and 1875 and was buffeted by a number of hurricanes. On August 31, 1886, an earthquake shook the tower.

Eleven men served as lighthouse keepers between 1862 and 1886, and George T. Clifford was keeper from 1886 to 1917. The lighthouse received electric power in the late 1930s, and the Coast Guard took possession of it in 1939. The lighthouse was manned until 1965, when it was automated. The possibility that the old lighthouse might be razed to reduce the risk to jets using a nearby airfield led to the establishment in 1971 of the Gulf Islands National Seashore, which preserved Fort Barrancas, Fort Pickens, and the Pensacola Lighthouse. The lighthouse keepers' duplex has been lovingly restored to its 1880s' appearance.

A wealth of evidence proves that the Pensacola Lighthouse is haunted. Pensacola resident Emmit Hatten, who lived in the keepers' quarters from 1931 to 1953, first suspected that he and his family were sharing the house with one of the former residents when he was ten years old. He was awakened

The first lighthouse keeper was stabbed to death by his wife inside the Pensacola Lighthouse in 1840.

by his mother to investigate a creaking sound on the stairway. He stood at the top of the stairs and yelled, "Who's there?" but received no reply. He then heard the front door open and close. He peered out of the balcony window just in time to see the yard gate open and close. Years later, when he was in the tower by himself, pulling on the chains that rotated the lens, he heard someone breathing behind him.

In the late 1980s, a worker climbed up the tower's 177 steps to fix the light, which had gone out. Meanwhile, his wife, who was waiting on the first floor of the visitor's center, heard a male voice cursing loudly. It definitely wasn't her husband's voice. The cursing stopped when the beacon came on. In 1994 a couple of workmen discovered that a rope had been wrapped around the water pipes on the second floor as insulation back in 1937. The men tried unsuccessfully to remove the rope and left. The next day, they were shocked to find the same rope draped around a light fixture in the shape of a hangman's noose. A few years later, a woman and her daughter were walking outside the tower one evening when they saw a woman in a white dress walking on the catwalk at the top of the lighthouse. The revolving light passed right through her.

Tour guides say that a heavy hatch door to the lantern room occasionally slams shut when no one is around. They have heard women's voices and footsteps on the second floor of the keepers' house and have felt cold air cascading over them, even on very hot days. A visitor once told a tour guide that she felt a disembodied hand on her shoulder. Another visitor said that someone unseen pulled her hair. Several tour guides have heard a spectral voice calling their names when they've been alone in the keepers' house. Some have even seen the ghost of a slave boy in the basement, hiding behind the staircase.

A formal investigation of the Pensacola Lighthouse was held on September 23, 2012, by members of several paranormal groups who were able to capture an EVP of two interactive ghosts. When one of the investigators asked, "Are you jumping on the bed?," she recorded the voice of a little boy saying "No." When she asked the same question again, she recorded a little girl's voice saying "Yes." In addition, several of the investigators had personal experiences. All of the women who were taking readings in the basement came down with splitting headaches. Investigators Richard Valdes and a female colleague actually saw a full-bodied apparition: "My colleague witnessed a small, shadowy figure run down the hallway. She followed it into the living room. I then followed her. We both witnessed the same apparition. It appeared to be the size of a child. It was standing between the liquor cabinet and a display case. I was trying to verify with her what we were seeing. I said, 'Can you tell me how high it was?' She told me it was child-sized, and I said, "OK, I saw the same thing.' When my colleague checked her voice recorder, which was running at the time, it had dropped to one bar. Something definitely drained her battery." Richard said this was only the second time in his ghost-hunting career that he has seen an apparition as clear as this one.

Because the true source of the haunting of the Pensacola Lighthouse is unknown, folklore has stepped in to provide the answer. Emmit Hatten said that keeper Jeremiah Ingraham was stabbed to death by his wife, Michaela, in 1840. Bloodstains on the floor of a bedroom supposedly bear mute testimony to the alleged murder. However, the blood could have come from the wounds of soldiers who were treated there during the Civil War. It also may have come from a woman named Ella who gave birth inside the keepers' house. The story of Jeremiah Ingraham's demise might be apocryphal, but logic can't explain all of the sightings and personal experiences that have taken place in the Pensacola Lighthouse over the years.

Chapter Fourteen

Safety Harbor

Safety Harbor Spa

For more than two thousand years, human beings have been living in the area where the Safety Harbor Spa is located. The first inhabitants were the Indian shell mound builders, who were replaced by the Tocobaga Indians and the Seminoles. White Europeans didn't arrive until 1539, when Spanish explorer Hernando De Soto sailed into Tampa Bay and discovered natural springs that he believed were the fabled Fountain of Youth, which he believed the expedition led by Ponce de Leon had failed to find. De Soto named the springs *Espiritu Santo Springs,* or Springs of the Holy Spirit. In the 1850s, a veteran of the Second Seminole War, Colonel William J. Bailey, bought the springs from the U.S. government. People desperate to find a miracle cure for their ailments flocked to the area the first owner called Bailey by the Sea. They were lured to the mineral springs by stories of people like Jesse Green, a farmer who regained the ability to walk and work in his fields after drinking the springs' water.

In the late nineteenth and early twentieth centuries, Safety Harbor was promoted as a health resort whose springs offered visitors relief from skin, kidney, and general health problems. The water from one of the springs was even bottled and sold. In the 1920s, the property passed into the hands of Captain James F. Tucker and his wife, Virginia. They built the Safety Harbor Sanitarium and the Espiritu Santo Springs

Hotel, which is known today as the Harbor House. In 1936 the Tuckers sold the springs and the surrounding land to Dr. Alben Jansik and his wife to pay their back taxes. The Jansiks repaired the resort and dug a 45-by-95-foot swimming pool. Through their massive publicity campaign, they attracted people from all over the county, including Harry Houdini and department store owner Russ Kresge.

The resort became a world-renowned place of healing after Dr. Salem H. Baranoff bought the springs and sanitarium in 1945. He enlisted the services of two other doctors and by 1950 had created a true health spa and resort that offered guests steam and mineral baths and massages. The Safety Harbor Spa attracted thousands of snowbirds from the Midwest who sought relaxation and relief from suffering. Athletes also traveled to the resort to benefit from the springs' curative powers and to participate in training camp.

The Safety Harbor Spa was designated a historical landmark in 1964 by the U.S. Department of the Interior and was named a Florida Heritage Landmark in 1997. In 2004 the spa was purchased by the Olympia Development Group of Dunedin, Florida. The new owners have maintained Safety Harbor Spa's reputation as a place where guests may partake of the soothing qualities of the mineral springs while broadening the resort's focus to include a conference center and a wellness center. Inadvertently, Safety Harbor Spa has also acquired a reputation as a place where you can get in touch with the paranormal.

In the book *Ghost Stories of Clearwater & St. Petersburg*, author Kim Cool says that a number of unexplained occurrences have created mayhem inside the old spa. Ghostly piano playing has been heard inside the former dining room. A guest who was eating in the dining room felt someone breathing down her neck even though her back was to a wall. A former night manager frequently received telephone calls from rooms that hadn't been booked for the night. She always asked security guards to investigate, but the rooms were empty. The guards did say, though, that they heard someone talking inside the room before they opened the door.

Dr. Baranoff also seems to be making his presence known in his beloved spa. Because he was a teetotaler, he has been credited with making the corks pop off bottles of wine. Since he believed that people used far too much salt, his ghost is blamed when salt shakers go missing. Dr. Baranoff's full-bodied apparition also makes an occasional appearance. In the book *Ghost Stories of St. Petersburg, Clearwater and Pinellas County*, author Deborah Frethem says that the ghost of the gray-haired doctor has been seen near the old oak tree that bears his name and near the springs, where he still asks guests how they're feeling.

Interestingly enough, the Safety Harbor Spa also seems to have a haunted bronze dog statue, which has been known to move to different spots inside the hotel during the night. Two guests even claim to have been bitten by the statue. Even though people claim that petting the statue might cause you to be haunted, guests are still attracted to the dog, especially children. The same can be said about Safety Harbor Spa itself, which continues to attract guests, even though they might bump into a ghost during their stay.

Chapter Fifteen

Sarasota

The Ringling College of Art and Design

T he Ringling College of Art and Design was the brainchild of Dr. Ludd M. Spivey, the president of Southern College. Dr. Spivey proposed the idea of the art school, originally conceived as a branch of the college, to John Ringling of the Ringling Brothers and Barnum & Bailey Circus. Ringling, who was nearly broke at the time, agreed to establish the art school in conjunction with the art museum he had built to showcase his collection of seventeenth-century artwork. The nexus of the new art school was the abandoned Bay Haven Hotel and several adjacent buildings, all of which were located close to Ringling's museum on 33rd Street. Ringling agreed to raise the $45,000 needed to renovate the buildings.

On October 2, 1931, the School of Fine and Applied Art of the John and Mable Ringling Art Museum officially opened its doors. Dr. Spivey selected Verman Kimbrough as the school's residential director. During its first year of operation, seventy-five students attended, each paying $432 for tuition and $315 for room and board. The first class could choose from 111 courses taught by 13 instructors, one of whom was Dr. Laura Ganno-McNeill, the first woman in the United States to receive a Ph.D. Because monies from the Ringling School of Art were being used to pay the salaries of the faculty of Southern College, the faculty at Ringling received very little compensation. The situation was remedied when President Kimbrough convinced John Ringling that the school should be divorced from Southern College. In 1933 the Ringling School of Art became an independent institution as well as a member of the Florida Association of Colleges and Universities.

Today Ringling College of Art and Design is a private, nonprofit institution offering bachelor's degrees in fourteen subject areas. Ninety buildings are situated on the thirty-five-acre campus, but the most persistent legend associated with Ringling College centers around one of the school's oldest buildings, the Bay Haven Hotel, which was converted into an administrative building and dormitory called Keating Hall.

In the late 1920s, when the building was still a hotel, a number of prostitutes plied their trade on the second floor. Their customers were generally businessmen who spent the night at the hotel. One of these ladies of the night was a young woman known today only as Mary. Legend has it that Mary fell hopelessly in love with one of her customers, who was married. Because he was unwilling to abandon his wife and family for her, Mary decided that life wasn't worth living. One night, she walked up to the third floor of the hotel and tied one end of a curtain rope around the rail of the staircase and the other end around her neck. She then climbed on top of the rail and jumped, breaking her neck. The other girls stared in horror as Mary's body slowly swayed back and forth.

According to Greg Jenkins, author of *Florida's Ghostly Legends and Haunted Folklore*, Mary's tragic end has given rise to a number of ghost stories, making Keating Hall one of the most haunted campus buildings in the United States. Mary's spectral image has appeared in one of the second-floor windows, staring down at passing students. Most witnesses describe her as an attractive young woman in her late teens or early twenties. Some say she is dressed in the style of the 1920s with a skullcap on her head. Others say she wears a cream-colored, ruffled dress. Some students, however, describe her as a skeletal figure with stringy hair and a tattered, rotten dress. Since the 1990s, the manifestations of the ghostly prostitute have been much less defined. She is now merely a shadowy form that follows students down the hall. As soon as someone catches sight of her, she vanishes into the now-closed-off stairwell.

Poltergeist activity has also been reported in Keating Hall. Students report hearing their doorknobs rattle late at night. Hallway lights and electrical devices turn on and off by themselves. Footsteps are heard in the women's restroom. Objects placed in one spot at night show up in an entirely different location the next morning. Mary's ghost could be responsible for the paranormal activity that has been reported in the classrooms as well. One student woke up early one morning to work on a painting. She had just set up her easel in the classroom when she heard someone knock on the door. She opened the door, but no one was in the hallway so she turned around. To her surprise, a large fan moved across the floor a few inches, several stools began moving on their own, and the paper towel dispenser began rolling out paper. She was so frightened that she ran from the classroom back to the dorm.

Today's student population at Ringling College is far different from the first class of students who arrived on campus in 1931. The thirteen hundred plus students hail from forty-three states and twenty-three foreign countries. Students and faculty would probably agree, though, that the most fascinating person on campus isn't even alive.

The Florida Studio Theatre

The building in which the Florida Studio Theatre is housed was originally the home of the Sarasota Woman's Club. The Tudor Revival structure was designed by architect H.N. Hall and built by contractor George Lysat in 1915 at a cost of $4,500. Sarasota's library was also housed within the clubhouse. Fundraisers kept the Woman's Club going until 1940, when it became public. After club member Naomi Widrig remodeled the clubhouse, the building was rededicated in 1953 and was designated a historical site in 1977. In 1982 Joe and Marian McKenna paid Boomhauer Reality $100,000 for the old clubhouse just before it was scheduled to be demolished to make room for a parking lot. They leased the building rent-free to the Florida Studio Theatre, and it's the oldest building currently being used as a theater in Sarasota. Since 1982, the old clubhouse has been extensively renovated. The main stage—the 173-seat Keating Theatre—attracts more than 175,000 people annually.

The hauntings at the Florida Studio Theatre are not nearly as well known as the more dramatic paranormal disturbances at the University of Tampa's Falk Theatre (discussed in a later chapter). Still, enough bizarre occurrences took place at the Florida Studio Theatre that members of the stage crew went nowhere in the building alone. In her book *Ghost Stories of Sarasota*, author Kim Cool says that soon after the theater opened in 1982, reports surfaced of strange rapping sounds and objects falling off tables for no apparent reason. People became so afraid to be there that the artistic director, Richard Hopkins, and his assistant, Kate Alexander, hired a couple of spiritualists to cleanse the theater. After the women burned incense and candles and rang bells, the reports of paranormal activity within the theater declined dramatically.

Sarasota Opera House

Arthur Britton (A.B.) Edwards was an important figure in Sarasota's history. He was the first real estate broker and the city's first mayor. By the mid 1920s, Edwards decided that a city of Sarasota's size needed a true cultural center so he hired architect Roy A. Jackson to design a multipurpose building that would be suitable for opera, movies, and other forms of entertainment. Edwards was certain it would become the nucleus of the growing resort town with its cream-colored stucco exterior and ornamental plasterwork. All three floors surrounded a central atrium. Eight shops were housed on the first floor; twelve offices occupied the second floor. The auditorium took up the rest of the building. A Robert Morton orchestral pipe organ was the auditorium's most impressive feature.

The Mediterranean Revival–style opera house opened its doors on April 10, 1926, featuring the silent film *Skinner's Dress Suit,* starring Reginald Denny and Laura LaPlante. Throughout the 1920s and 1930s, the opera house offered first-class entertainment, including Will Rogers, Sally Rand, the Ziegfeld Follies, Tom Mix, W.C. Fields, and Elvis Presley. A.B. Edwards Opera House also hosted the world premiere of Cecil B. Demille's *The Greatest Show on Earth,* which was filmed in Sarasota.

The A.B. Edwards Opera House has undergone a number of transformations throughout its history. The theater's appearance changed along with its name to the Florida Theater. Many of its original Art Deco furnishings were replaced with plastic, laminate, and linoleum. In 1928 a hurricane destroyed the Robert Morton pipe organ. In 1973 the old theater closed its doors.

The building stood empty for several years. Then in 1979, the newly formed Asolo Opera Guild bought the Edwards Theater for $150,000. The remodeling of the orchestra pit and the stage were completed in 1984, just in time for the theater's first production, *Eugene Onegin*. Repairs to the balcony were finished in 1990; three years later, the lobby and façade were restored. In the mid 1990s, an adjacent building was converted into the Pavilion, which houses the Peterson Great Room, the Jonas Kamlet Library, and the Culverhouse Room. In 2007 the auditorium was entirely gutted so the orchestra pit could be deepened. The backstage area was remodeled as well.

Some employees believe that all of the renovations have inadvertently awakened a dormant spirit within the old opera house. One longtime staff member told Kim Cool, author of *Ghost Stories of Sarasota*, that he believes the building is haunted by the ghost of a theater guest who walks through the Peterson Great Room in the Pavilion building late at night. The employee usually hears the spirit's disembodied footsteps between 11:30 P.M. and midnight. Most theater lovers would probably agree with the ghost of the Sarasota Opera House that there are worse places to spend eternity.

The Players Theatre

The Players Theatre is the oldest theater in Sarasota. In the mid 1930s, the theater group was a loosely formed collection of budding actors and actresses looking for a permanent home. In 1936 the Players Theatre moved into an old theater at the corner of Tamiami Trail and 9th Street. The building, constructed mostly of cypress, had 246 seats and a theatrical lighting system. In the early 1970s, the original theater was replaced by the current building, which can seat five hundred people. A number of well-known actors and actresses have appeared on the theater's stage, including Montgomery Clift, Jayne Meadows, Polly Holiday, and Charlton Heston. Ironically, the person who has made the most lasting impression on the Players Theatre is a little-known actress named Lauren Melville.

According to author Kim Cool, in 1997 Lauren Melville was a young actress with a promising career ahead of her. She had just received favorable reviews for her performance in a production of *How to Succeed in Business Without Really Trying* at the Venice Theatre. She had gone to a party and was relaxing on the lawn of the host's house with two other friends when a drunk driver, sixteen-year-old Mark Chapman, slammed his car into another car, which careened into the group of friends. Lauren was killed instantly; the other young people were transported by helicopter to Bayfront Medical Center in St. Petersburg.

Not long after Lauren's tragic death, Robert Atkins, one of the actors in a production of *Call Me Madame*, arrived at the theater thirty minutes before rehearsals were scheduled to begin. He walked onto the stage and noticed an attractive young woman standing on stage right. He left the stage and took care of some unfinished business. When he returned, the girl was standing on stage left. Atkins asked her if she needed any help, and she said no. Atkins then went to a nearby dressing room. For ten minutes, he kept glancing over at the stage to see if the girl was still there. After a while, she was gone. A week later, Atkins was in the dressing room when he noticed a small photograph of the girl stuck in a mirror being used by Lauren's boyfriend, Steve Dawson, whose face blanched when Atkins informed him that he had seen Lauren in the theater the week before.

Apparently, Lauren Melville is not the only spirit haunting the Players Theater. Loren Mayo, a writer for the *Sarasota Observer*, said that in the late 2000s, a costume designer noticed four old women sitting in the first few rows of the theater. They were wearing old-fashioned dresses and talking among themselves. They completely ignored the costume designer when she asked them what they were doing there. The angry woman marched down the steps of the stage, determined to get the ladies' attention. Just before she reached their seats, they vanished.

According to Troy Taylor, author *of The Ghost Hunter's Handbook*, theaters are one of the best places to find ghosts. He suspects that the high emotions of the actors imprint themselves on the buildings themselves. Sometimes the spirits are reanimated, like a film loop that plays over and over again. Because these spirits don't interact with the living, they fall into the category of what paranormal investigators call residual hauntings.

A much younger ghost is roaming the old theater as well. In 2009 the artistic director, Jeffrey Kin, was standing backstage when he saw a pair of small hands pressing into a transparent curtain. Thinking that one of the stagehands had brought one of his children to the theater, Kin questioned the man and was puzzled when the stagehand asserted he had left all of his children home that day. Not long thereafter, psychic Rosemary Altea attended a production of *Smile*. Afterwards, she informed Kin that the child was the ghost of his younger brother, who was stillborn. The baby had taken the form of an older child to get Kin's attention to appeal to him not to work so hard. The child was, the psychic said, not as much a ghost as a guardian angel.

The ghost stories piqued the interest of a local paranormal group called Ghosthunters of SRQ, who conducted a formal investigation of the theater in 2011. Three of the members were walking down a main aisle when a light illuminating the stage went off by itself. Other members were on their way to the prop room when two of their walkie-talkies rang, but no one was on the other end of the line. The theater's managing director, Michelle Bianchi Pingel, accompanied the group on their investigation and revealed her own experience. Years earlier, she was in the costume loft when several dresses hanging on a rack moved on their own as if an invisible hand had pushed them.

126

Chapter Sixteen

St. Petersburg

The Vinoy Hotel

The Vinoy Hotel is St. Petersburg's most recognizable landmark whose inception happened in the home of land developer Aymer Vinoy Laughner. In 1924, during one of Laughner's parties, he discussed with another land developer, Eugene Elliot, and pro golfer Walter Hagen his dream of building a huge hotel in St. Petersburg. During a lull in the party, the three men walked out to the front yard to hit a few golf balls. Before they teed off, Hagen told Laughner that he was going to put his commitment to building a new hotel to the test and asked him for his pocket watch. Placing the watch on the ground, Hagen asked Laughner if he would like to make a wager: If he could hit three golf balls off Laughner's watch without breaking the crystal, Laughner would have to put up his share of the money to build the hotel in the exact spot where the balls landed. Laughner agreed, and Hagen proceeded to hit the three golf balls into an orange grove several hundred yards away, leaving the watch crystal intact. The next morning, the three men pooled their resources and bought the property from a Mr. Williamson. Legend has it that they signed the contract on a paper bag. According to Laughner's building permit, he had to complete construction of the hotel by the end of 1925. With only ten months to make his dream hotel a reality, Laughner ordered architect Henry Taylor to push his workmen to the limit. They came through with no time to spare. The grand opening of the Vinoy was held on December 31, 1925. Elliot suggested naming the hotel the Vinoy "because it is such a pretty name."

Thousands of tourists, attracted by Florida's burgeoning reputation as the country's vacation mecca, booked rooms in the Vinoy Hotel in the 1920s and 1930s, paying what was then the exorbitant rate of $20 per night. In the beginning, the Vinoy was open only from December to March, and the red light in the tower was turned on only during vacation season. The rich and famous basked in the Vinoy's tropical splendor during the hotel's heyday, including Jimmy Stewart, Babe Ruth, and Presidents Calvin Coolidge and Herbert Hoover.

The Vinoy underwent a series of dramatic changes in the 1940s. In 1942 Laughner leased the hotel to the U.S. War Department, which used it for training purposes. In 1944 the War Department canceled its agreement with Laughner, and in 1945 Laughner sold the Vinoy to Charles Alberling for $700,000. Although the Vinoy prospered under Alberling's ownership at first, by the 1970s the cost of an overnight stay had dropped from $50 to $7. The saddest period in the Vinoy's history began in 1975, when all of its beautiful furnishings were sold and its doors were closed. For the next fourteen years, the only occupants were vagrants and pigeons. Three feet of water stood in the basement. Many of the windows were broken. The stench from the abandoned wreck was said to be so bad that people went out of their way to avoid walking past the building. Ironically, the Vinoy was placed on the National Register of Historic Places in 1978.

The dilapidated state of what was once the "crown jewel of St. Petersburg" moved a group of citizens to campaign for the Vinoy's restoration. It was saved from utter destruction in

1989, when the Federal Construction Company was awarded a $33.6-million contract to restore the old hotel to its former glory. The new owner, the Vinoy Development Corporation, opened the doors of the extensively remodeled Stouffer Vinoy Hotel in 1992. The cost of the restoration was said to exceed $100 million. Longtime residents of St. Petersburg swore that the new Vinoy was almost an exact replica of the fabulous hotel that welcomed its first guests on New Year's Eve of 1925. Four years later, the Renaissance Vinoy Resort was taken over by a Hong Kong–based corporation, CTF. In 1997 the Vinoy changed owners again when it was purchased by Marriott International. Following a $4-million restoration of the rooms in 2004, the Vinoy is now a four-diamond hotel, the pride of St. Petersburg.

Guest and staff members began talking about possible paranormal activity in the Vinoy only one year after its doors opened. As early as 1926, people reported the appearance of weird figures in the tower, which is always locked, and a woman in white on the fifth floor. The latter spirit could be one of two women: Elsie Elliot or Annie Gadsen. In 1926 Eugene Elliot was under a great deal of stress. His business was in decline, and he owed $500,000 in back taxes. Then his wife, Elsie, informed him that she was going to divorce him. Elliot snapped. He pushed her down the stairs in their family home. Elsie hit her head on the floor and later died in the bedroom. The Elliots' maid, Annie, told the police that she witnessed Elsie's violent end, and Elliot was arrested. However, before the trial began, Annie disappeared.

In her book *Ghost Stories of Clearwater & St. Petersburg*, author Kim Cool writes about the lilting sounds of a waltz filtering from the Vinoy ballroom, which has hosted hundreds of dances and wedding receptions over the years. Cool speculates that the music may be produced by the spirits of bandleader Paul Whiteman and his orchestra, who performed at the Vinoy during its grand opening gala. Spectral music is a type of residual haunting commonly found in theaters, auditoriums, and concert halls.

For years, baseball teams undergoing spring training have visited the Vinoy Hotel. For more than a decade, the hotel has hosted visiting teams playing against the Tampa Bay Devil Rays. The Vinoy's haunted reputation received national attention when ESPN ran a story about Scott Williamson, a relief pitcher for the Cincinnati Reds, who had a paranormal encounter in June 2003. As he was getting ready for bed, a tingling sensation spread throughout his body. He felt as if someone was watching him, even though he was certain he was alone. He fell asleep and was sleeping on his back when he woke up, unable to breathe, as if pressure was being placed on his chest. Williamson rolled over onto his stomach and was

Baseball players have had ghostly visitations while spending the night at the Vinoy Hotel.

able to breathe again. After a few minutes, however, he felt once again as if someone was sitting on top of him, making breathing almost impossible. As he rolled onto his back again, he saw a man dressed in either 1940s' or 1950s' clothing standing in front of the curtains. After Williamson's story ran on ESPN, a friend researched the history of the Vinoy and informed him that a man who was also named Williamson died in the hotel.

The next day, the Cincinnati Reds checked out of the Vinoy and the Pittsburgh Pirates checked in. Strength and pitching coordinator Frank Velasquez plopped into bed 3:00 A.M. and fell asleep almost instantly. He was awakened two hours later by the feeling that he wasn't alone. He opened his eyes and was surprised to see a sandy-haired man standing by a desk in front of a window. Velasquez observed that the man was wearing a white shirt and khaki pants, but after his eyes focused he realized that the man was transparent. Velasquez rolled over and went back to sleep, attributing the hallucination to fatigue. The next day, teammate Craig Wilson told Velasquez about the ESPN story detailing Scott Williamson's ghostly encounter the day before. Goosebumps rose on Velasquez's arms when he realized that he didn't imagine the appearance of the strange man in his room.

A formal investigation of the Vinoy was conducted by the Atlantic Paranormal Society (TAPS) in 2008. During their four-day investigation, the members collected some startling evidence. Jason Hawes was asleep when a fold-up ironing board in the closet pushed the door open. The incident was recorded on video. The next day, Hawes and Grant Wilson tried unsuccessfully to get the ironing board to push the closet door open. During another night in the room, Hawes heard voices coming from the same closet.

The Beach Drive Inn

The white stucco house at 532 Beach Drive was probably built around 1910. The exact date of its construction is unknown because most of the city's titles and deeds were burned in a fire in the county courthouse in 1913. Most of the early owners of the house were real estate developers, such as C.R. Hall, who owned the house between 1914 and 1916, and William Petten, who lived there in 1918. The most famous owner, however, was Aymer Vinoy Laughner, who bought the house in 1919. Laughner and his family continued living in their comparatively modest home for many years. Aymer died in 1961, wife Stella in 1976. In 2007 the old house was converted into a bed-and-breakfast called the Beach Drive Inn. At the time, new owners Roland and Heather didn't realize that the

Guests report that the ghost of a drunken maid still rocks in her rocking chair at the Beach Drive Inn.

house came with the ghost of a former employee.

One of the six rooms that the new owners redecorated is called the Montego Room. In the first half of the twentieth century, a maid who worked for the Laughner family lived in this room. At the end of the day, the maid drank herself insensible while sitting in her rocking chair. When Aymer Laughner learned of the maid's late-night tippling, he fired her. In her book *Ghost Stories of St. Petersburg, Clearwater and Pinellas County,* author Deborah Frethem says that guests staying in the Montego Room have detected a female presence watching their every move. The former maid's rocking chair has been known to rock by itself at times, and the shadowy figure of the maid was seen on one of the walls in the room.

The Beach Drive Inn's hauntings have received publicity in recent years. The bed-and-breakfast has been featured on two paranormal-themed television shows on the Discovery Channel: *Psychic Kids* and *Children of the Paranormal,* garnering it the attention of paranormal investigators.

St. Petersburg High School

When St. Petersburg High School was built in 1926 at 701 Mirror Lake Drive, it was said to be the first million-dollar high school in the United States. Designed in the Spanish Mission Revival style, the school contains many of the architectural elements common among buildings built during the 1920s' boom era. The exterior of the school is coated with a stucco surface embedded with multicolored Chattahoochee stones.

The building served as a high school from 1931 to 1964, then became the St. Petersburg Girl's Junior High School. From 1967 to 1985, the Mirror Lake Adult Education Center was housed in the building. In 1991 St. Petersburg High School was converted into a condominium. Some people say that a few ghosts occupy the former hallowed halls of learning.

Rumors that school was haunted began surfacing in the 1940s. Students, faculty, and support staff reported hearing scratching and scurrying sounds on the third and fourth floors and seeing lights flickering on and off. Electricians summoned to the school were unable to locate the source of the problem.

Many people have seen dark figures strolling down the hallways and passing through closed doors. Witnesses have described the specters as small, almost child-size. The ghost of a sixteen-year-old boy with a crew cut has been known to manifest on the third and fourth floors between 11:00 P.M. and 4:00 or 5:00 A.M. He is usually seen wearing dark pants and a white sweatshirt with a dark stripe across the middle. He walks with his head bowed, as if deep in thought. He has also been seen staring out of the windows on the upper floors.

Jungle Park

From 900 A.D. to the 1500s, the Tocobaga Indians lived at the northern end of Tampa Bay in round houses supported by wooden poles and covered with palm thatch. The temple and the tribal chief's hut were erected on top of mounds composed of shells, earth, and rock. The Tocobaga also built burial mounds in the area, as well as smaller mounds called middens, which were created when the tribe threw fish bones and clamshells into garbage heaps. The Tocobaga also feasted on rabbits, squirrels, deer, berries, nuts, and fruit. Their peaceful existence was disrupted in 1528 when Spanish explorer Panfilo de Narvaez arrived in the region in search of gold. Predictably, confrontations between the European invaders and the indigenous inhabitants erupted in violence. Within one hundred years after the arrival of the conquistadors, the Tocobaga Indians were extinct.

One Tocobaga village was located between Park Street and 17th Avenue North on Boca Ciega Bay. The first land developer to take an interest in this part of St. Petersburg was H. Walter Fuller. Born in Atlanta in 1865, Fuller traveled to the Tampa Bay area and raised oranges. By 1886 Fuller was owner and operator of an electric streetcar company in Bradenton. In 1909 he began extending his streetcar line from 9th Street to Boca Ciega. By 1913 his trolley line stretched seven miles down Central Avenue to a wilderness area Fuller called the "jungle." Because Fuller facilitated travel throughout the Tampa Bay area, he is generally credited with initiating St. Petersburg's first land boom from 1911 to 1914.

H. Walter Fuller's son, Walter P. Fuller, continued his father's efforts to develop the jungle. After he paved sixteen miles of city streets, he built the Jungle Hotel at Park Street and 5th Avenue North to accommodate the influx of tourists to the area. Between 1923 and 1924, Fuller built St. Petersburg's first shopping plaza, Jungle Prada, which included a speakeasy called the Gangplank. Gangsters like Al Capone used the Jungle Hotel's airport when they visited the Gangplank. During Prohibition, bootleggers delivered booze to the Gangplank through a secret tunnel leading from Tampa Bay to the jungle. Music was provided by some of the best-known performers of the day, like Count Basie and Duke Ellington.

The passing of time has brought change to the jungle. Most of the Indian mounds on Park Street have been leveled to make space for housing. Jungle Park property was taken over by the city of St. Petersburg in 1970 to prevent further development. The Gangplank is gone; a restaurant called

Saffron's Caribbean Cuisine has taken its place in the old Jungle Prada shopping center. Adjacent to Jungle Park is the Sacred Lands Preservation and Education Center, where an Indian mound has been carefully preserved. The mound where the chief's house sat is gone; an artist's studio now sits on the spot. Some locals believe that the traditional rituals practiced at Sacred Lands by teachers and spiritual leaders—as well as the archaeological digs conducted by the Florida Central Gulf Coast Archaeological Society in the mid 1990s—have awakened some of the spirits that had lain dormant for centuries.

For many years, sightings of the spirits of Spanish explorers and peaceful Tocobaga Indians have been reported in Jungle Park. An article appearing in a 1972 edition of the *St. Petersburg Independent* reported ghostly activity in a condemned house at 1699 Park Street. In his book *Ghost Stories of St. Petersburg, Florida,* author Tim Resser says that employees at Saffron's Caribbean Cuisine tell stories about a ghost they call the gray lady. A waitress named Wanda was closing the restaurant late one night when she saw a woman walk past a potted plant in the direction of the parking lot. Wanda went over to the bartender to tell him what she had seen. Suddenly, the specter reappeared, walking in the opposite direction. Workers were so upset about the weird disturbances inside the restaurant that the owner, Edyth, performed a ritual to expel unwanted spirits. Although the paranormal activity has decreased, rumors persist about the spirits of Al Capone and his cronies wandering around the former speakeasy. Although the Tocobaga Indians no longer live and worship at Jungle Park, it is still in many ways a spiritual place.

Flori de Leon Apartments

The Flori de Leon Apartments were the first cooperative on
Florida's west coast. The seven-story, Mediterranean Revival–
style apartment complex was erected in 1926, just a few
months after the Vinoy Hotel was built. Flori de Leon was
built in the shape of an H to enhance ventilation, with a large
courtyard in front and a smaller courtyard in back. Cement
benches allow residents to take in the beauty of the water
fountain and the intricate landscaping. Two large lounge areas,

The spirits of Lou Gehrig and Babe Ruth still reside at the Flori de Leon Apartments.

each with an adjoining roof deck, are on the top floor. Today the Flori de Leon offers condominiums to people at lease fifty-five years old, but its most famous residents died many years ago.

In the early 1930s, the Flori de Leon Apartments were the temporary home of New York Yankees star players Lou Gehrig and Babe Ruth. Gehrig leased Apartment 701, Ruth Apartment 702. People living in Apartment 701 have sensed the presence of a sad and lonely spirit. However, people living near Apartment 702 have been awakened in the middle of the night by the sounds of raucous laughter and loud music, even when Ruth's penthouse is vacant. The noise is said to carry all the way to the bottom floor.

The Mansion House

The first owner of the bungalow at 105 Fifth Avenue Northeast was St. Petersburg's first mayor, David Moffett. Born in 1842 near Bloomington, Indiana, Moffett arrived in Pinellas County in 1882, making his home in Point Pinellas Post Office, the original name of St. Petersburg. On February 29, 1892, St. Petersburg was incorporated as a town, and Moffett was elected mayor on an anti-saloon ticket. Moffett narrowly defeated the founder of St. Petersburg, John Williams, who died a few weeks later. After serving a single term as mayor, Moffett became superintendent of schools as well as a deacon of the First Congregational Church. Throughout his life, Moffett believed that alcohol was the root of most of society's problems, and he worked tirelessly to make Prohibition a reality. Moffett died of a stroke in 1921 and was buried in Greenwood Cemetery.

Moffett's house, which was built in 1904, was coated with stucco on the first floor exterior. The exterior of the second floor was covered with peach-colored shingle siding.

The awnings and trim were painted green. The house next door, which is the mirror image of Moffett's house, was built in 1912 for a Dr. Kemp. In the mid 1920s, both homes were purchased by Dr. R.K. O'Brien, who used one as his residence and the other as his office.

David Moffett's house passed through a variety of owners in the twentieth century. In the 1940s, it was owned by a doctor who specialized in the treatment of children with psychiatric problems. In the early 2000s, it was converted into a bed-and-breakfast by Kathy and Peter Plautz, who were from Wales. They named their business the Mansion House because in Wales, the word mansion refers to the mayor's house. Before long, guests began reporting strange experiences inside the old house. In her book *Ghost Stories of St. Petersburg, Clearwater and Pinellas County*, author Deborah Frethem says that guests

The Mansion House at 105 Fifth Avenue Northeast was the home of former mayor David Moffett.

who drank alcohol in their rooms sensed that someone was peering over their shoulders disapprovingly. A number of guests who sat in one of the big chairs on the first floor felt as if someone was breathing down their necks. During one of Deborah Frethem's ghost tours, my wife, Marilyn, took several photographs of a window on the second floor. The clear image of an orb appears in one of the photos.

The Mansion House is currently vacant and for sale at auction. The minimum bid was $200,000. Will the home's haunted reputation hamper or enhance its marketability?

The Coliseum Ballroom

The Coliseum Ballroom at 535 Fourth Avenue North has been called one of the finest dance halls in the entire South. It was built in 1924, just in time to take advantage of the increased flow of traffic made possible by the construction of the Gandy Bridge connecting St. Petersburg to Tampa. It cost $250,000—exorbitant at the time—and some of the biggest names of the Swing Era, including Benny Goodman, Tommy Dorsey, Glen Miller, and Guy Lombardo, appeared on the Coliseum's marquee. One musician who performed at the Coliseum was a banjo player named Rex McDonald, who started out playing with the Coliseum's house band, the Tom Danks Orchestra, in 1924. Two years later, he formed his own band, the Silver Kings. In the 1930s, he was made general manager of the Coliseum, and in 1944 he became the owner. He operated the dance hall with his wife, Thelma "Boo" McDonald, whom he married in 1932. Under their ownership, the Coliseum expanded its offerings to include auto shows, banquets, indoor sports events, and expositions. The couple was a fixture at the Coliseum until Rex's death in 1984. Thelma ran the business by herself for five years but finally sold it to the city of St. Petersburg in 1989.

Owning and operating the Coliseum Ballroom was a labor of love for Rex McDonald. According to the night watchmen, he is still supervising its daily operation. Phantom footsteps echo through the building during the late night and early morning hours. Sometimes it sounds as if someone is walking right next to a night watchman, keeping step with him, even though no one else is in the building. Rex McDonald, it seems, will always be as much a part of the Coliseum as its Mediterranean Revival–style architecture.

Chapter Seventeen

St. Petersburg Beach

Don Cesar Beach Resort

The story of the Pink Palace appeals to both die-hard romantics and lovers of ghost stories. Thomas Rowe was born in Boston, Massachusetts, in 1872. Orphaned at age four, Rowe was sent to England to be raised by his grandfather. As a young man, he was sent to school in London. In the early 1890s, he attended a performance of William Vincent Wallace's three-act opera *Maritana*. Rowe was transfixed by the dark-haired beauty who played the lead and after the performance introduced

The ghost of builder Thomas Rowe still longs for the love of his life, Lucinda, at the Don Cesar Hotel.

himself to the young woman, whose name was Lucinda. It was love a first sight for both of them. Rowe made frequent trips to London, meeting Lucinda by a special fountain in a private garden near the theater after her performances. After a few weeks, the couple planned to meet at the fountain at a designated time and elope in America. However, Lucinda's parents found out about their clandestine plans and forbade her to marry Rowe, largely on religious grounds. They sent Lucinda off to their country home in Spain, hoping that she would eventually forget about him. Rowe was heartbroken when his lover didn't meet him on the night they were scheduled to sail away to America. He settled in Norfolk, Virginia, and wrote to Lucinda, begging her to join him. All of his letters were returned, the seals unbroken.

Rowe eventually entered into a loveless marriage with a woman named Mary, but he still yearned for Lucinda. He became a successful land developer and threw himself into his work. Ten years later, Rowe received a letter from Lucinda's parents. Inside were Lucinda's obituary and a letter written in her own hand years before. Lucinda wrote that she would never forsake Thomas and that she would wait for him by their fountain. Tears streamed down Rowe's face as he read the letter, and he vowed that he would erect a grand hotel as a monument to Lucinda. He was forty-two years old and in poor health, but he was determined to make his dream a reality.

Leaving Mary behind, Rowe traveled to St. Petersburg Beach, where he bought a piece of land for $100,000. Constructing the hotel at this particular location was no easy task. All of the building materials had to be transported over a bridge owned by a man who charged Rowe for every single truckload. Rowe decided to paint the hotel's exterior pink, just like the Royal Hawaiian Hotel in Honolulu. Rowe named his hotel the Don Cesar Hotel after the leading man in *Maritana*. Approximately fifteen hundred guests attended the grand opening on January 16, 1928, including Franklin Delano Roosevelt and F. Scott and Zelda Fitzgerald. In the lobby, Rowe replicated the garden and the fountain where he and Lucinda rendezvoused in London.

People from all over the country stayed at the Don Cesar in its early years, even though it was open only in January and February. The Don Cesar even weathered the Great Depression, though business dropped off dramatically.

Thomas Rowe stayed in a penthouse suite in the hotel's early years, but as after his health declined he moved into an apartment behind the front desk. One day in 1940, he was standing in the lobby when he clutched his chest and collapsed. He was carried to Room 101, where he died of a heart attack.

After Rowe's death, the U.S. government bought the Don Cesar and converted it into a convalescent home for injured war veterans. Workers stripped the hotel of all of its lovely furnishings, bricked up windows, installed laminate over the marble floors, and painted the interior walls green. The contractor who was ordered in 1948 to destroy the fountain in the lobby hid a note under the floor. In the note, he provided a detailed description of the fountain and pinpointed its original location. When the Save the Don committee was formed in 1972 to restore the hotel, the note enabled artisans to create a duplicate of the original fountain. The Don Cesar Hotel reopened on November 29, 1973.

A number of different spirits have made the Don Cesar Hotel their permanent home. In her book *Ghost Stories of Clearwater & St. Petersburg*, author Kim Cool says that many people have seen the ghosts of a nurse wearing a white hat and an elderly man in a wheelchair. Guests staying on the second, sixth, and seventh floors have been awakened in the middle of the night by loud banging noises. People walking through the meeting rooms have seen a white figure moving around. Even the ghosts of Scott and Zelda Fitzgerald make an occasional appearance. The most commonly seen ghost in the Don Cesar, however, is the spirit of Thomas Rowe. Witnesses describe him as a figure in a white suit and a Panama hat who is often seen walking hand-in-hand with a beautiful, dark-eyed woman wearing a gypsy dress. Love, it seems, really is eternal.

Chapter Eighteen

Tampa

The Cuban Club

The Spanish-American War had a significant impact on the
Cuban population of Tampa Bay. At the end of the war in
1898, many Cubans living in Tampa Bay returned to Cuba, but
disillusionment brought on by the unfulfilled revolution set in,
and thousands returned to Tampa, determined to transform
Ybor City into their Havana away from home. This resurgence
of patriotic feeling in Tampa resulted in the formation of a
recreational society known as El Club Nacional Cuban on
October 10, 1899. In 1902 the three hundred members decided
to change the name of their organization to *El Circulo Cubano,*
or the Cuban Club. The club's formation, as expressed in the
charter of 1902, was "for the mutual benefit and enjoyment of
the members and for the charitable purposes and instruction
of its members and the dissemination of knowledge among all
classes of people." The first clubhouse was built on Fourteenth
Street and Tenth Avenue in 1907 at a cost of $18,000. It burned
down nine years later, and construction of a new clubhouse
began in 1917, thanks to a bond drive initiated by members.
When completed in 1918 at a cost of $60,000, the new building
featured a cantina, a pharmacy, a theater, and a library. With its
stained-glass windows and marble interior, the clubhouse was
deserving of its nickname, the Cathedral for Workers. Young
men and women were drawn to the clubhouse because of its
gymnasium, its boxing arena on the patio, and its seventy-by-

one-hundred-foot dance floor. Famous entertainers like Benny Moore and Celia Cruz performed there. Legend has it that even a bullfight was held at the Cuban Club years ago.

Membership has fluctuated dramatically over the years due to labor unrest and the vicissitudes of the cigar industry. Membership isn't nearly as restrictive as it was in the past. Members don't have to be of Cuban ancestry, but they do have to be committed to the principles on which the club was founded. Today the Cuban Club is rented out for events, features bands on the weekends, and even houses a couple of ghosts.

Two violent incidents from the Cuban Club's past have probably generated most of the hauntings in the old building. In the 1920s, an actor committed suicide on the stage of the theater. In the early 1930s, a number of members who were unhappy with the way the club was being managed formed a splinter group. One night in 1934 during a meeting at the club, an argument broke out. Fists flew and members pummeled each other in heaps on the floor. Suddenly several gunshots ripped through the air, and Bellarmino Vallejo lay on the floor, bleeding profusely. He had been shot in the face. By the time Bellarmino's elderly mother arrived at the clinic where he was being treated, he was dead. Overcome with grief, the woman collapsed on her son's prostrate body, wailing loudly.

The psychic impact of these two tragic deaths is said to have made an indelible impression on the old club. People have seen the apparition of a woman walking up a staircase, wearing a long, white dress and red high-heeled shoes. Witnesses have also seen a young boy playing with a ball in the area where the pool once was. Pale, spectral figures have been seen in the cantina. Male specters sporting suits and bowler hats and whistling popular tunes from years gone by occasionally show up in the elevators, which tend to move among the four floors of the building between 4:00 A.M. and 5:00 A.M. Policemen who were called to the Cuban Club to investigate a report of an intruder had an encounter with the ghost of a wailing women, probably the spirit of Vallejo's mother. A group of students from Hillsborough Community College ran out of the building after the piano they were looking at began playing by itself.

On another occasion, employees of the Cuban Club were making arrangements for a special event when they heard a female voice yell, "Help me! Help me!" Assuming that the voice belonged to a female coworker named Krista whom no one had seen all morning, they called her cell phone. Shock registered visibly on their faces when Krista told them that she had gotten up late and was just then pulling into the parking lot.

In 2009 the Atlantic Paranormal Society (TAPS) conducted a formal investigation at the Cuban Club for their SyFy television show *Ghost Hunters*. In the course of the evening, the group surmised that the building's close proximity to power lines could be causing people to have hallucinations. However, some of the night's events couldn't easily be explained. Disembodied footsteps were heard coming from the ballroom. A digital recorder picked up footsteps coming from the left staircase, where the woman in white has been seen. Using a flashlight, two team members made contact with the spirit of a little boy who plays in the basement. By night's end, TAPS reached the same conclusion that hundreds of visitors to the building have arrived at: The Cuban Club is indeed haunted.

The Tampa Theatre

The term "movie palace" is usually applied to large movie theaters built between the 1910s and the 1940s. The first true movie palace was the Mark Strand Theater, which was built in New York City in 1913. Between 1925 and 1930, hundreds of these lavishly decorated theaters opened every year. By the end of the 1920s, ninety million Americans were flocking to movie theaters every week. For only a dime, patrons could immerse themselves in elegance usually reserved for European royalty.

In the 1920s, architects favored classical, period-revival design and atmospheric design. A good example of an atmospheric theater is the 1926 Tampa Theatre. Architect John Eberson was trying to re-create a Mediterranean courtyard, but he also added Renaissance, Spanish, Greek Revival, Byzantine, English Tudor, and Baroque touches to the 1,446-seat theater.

For decades, the Tampa Theatre was the centerpiece of the cultural scene in Tampa. By the 1960s, however, attendance plummeted as people began fleeing to the suburbs, and the Tampa Theatre faced the same fate that had befallen hundreds of movie palaces across the country: an appointment with the wrecking ball. In 1973 Tampa residents petitioned to save the proud old theater. City leaders responded to the pressure and decided to assume the theater's leases. The Arts Council of Hillsborough agreed to renovate and manage the revived theater.

Programming included concerts, educational programs, tours, and, of course, films. Since 1978 more than five million people have attended events at the Tampa Theatre. In 1978 the theater was listed on the National Register of Historic Places, and it has also been designated a Tampa city landmark. The possibility that the old theater may be haunted has only added to the building's allure.

The Tampa Theatre's resident ghost is rumored to be the spirit of a former employee named Foster "Fink" Finley. In 1930 Fink was hired as a projectionist. He was, by all accounts, the consummate professional. Fink, a short, balding man, rode the bus, showing up for work every day at 8:00 A.M. even though the theater didn't open until 1:00 P.M. Fink began his workday by shaving and drinking a cup of *café con leche*. He was always seen wearing a suit and tie and smoking a cigarette. In 1965 Fink collapsed while operating the projector and died two months later. Some people say he died of a heart attack; others claim that cancer took his life. Regardless of the official cause of Fink's death, his chain-smoking was probably responsible for his health problems.

Poltergeist-like activity began occurring within the theater not long after Fink's death. Audience members claimed to have heard disembodied voices. Blasts of cold air have been felt throughout the building. Weird noises, such as the jingling of keys, have been heard in the projection booth. Doors open and close in areas where no one is present. People walking on the staircase that leads from the lobby and to the theater offices and bathrooms claim to have passed through cold spots. One night the power switch was shut off when no one was in the area. The faint scent of men's shaving lotion occasionally wafts through the air.

Some employees have had personal encounters with Fink's ghost. People opening or closing the theater have seen the figure of a man dressed in light colors. One worker was tapped on the shoulder by an invisible hand as he mopped the floor. The same worker had to make several trips to the shower room on the third floor to turn off a shower, which kept turning back on by itself. An employee who had just locked up the theater one Sunday afternoon heard a chain being dragged across the lobby floor. He opened the door to see who was inside, but the lobby was empty. The projectionist who took over Fink's position after he died was trying to close the door to the projection room late one night when he felt someone pulling on the door, preventing him from closing it. The projectionist released his hold on the door to see who wanted to enter, but no one was there. Several years ago, a projectionist who had left his knife in the projection booth was surprised to find it missing when he returned. On the suggestion of a friend, the projectionist asked Fink to return it. When he returned to the projection booth, he found his knife in a spot he had searched a few minutes before. Not all employees are amused by Fink's antics. One projectionist became so scared inside the small projection booth that he resigned the next day.

Not surprisingly, the Tampa Theatre has caught the attention of local ghost hunters. In 1984 a séance was held in the main auditorium, during which the participants sensed the presence of another person in the room. Then they heard the faint sound of music coming from the lobby. During the night, the image of a person appeared in the mirrors in front of the auditorium. In November 2009, the theater began offering Late-Night Ghost Hunts between 10:00 P.M. and 2:00 A.M. On the night of the first ghost tour, several guests reported that their newly charged batteries were drained just as they began their investigation. One of the guides was walking through the green room when two 9-volt batteries inside his backpack burned up. A number of visitors have caught orbs and mists with their digital cameras.

In 2005 the SPIRIT ghost team of St. Petersburg detected the presence of a second entity inside the theater. A psychic who was accompanying the group claimed to have made contact with the ghost of a woman named Jezebel or Jesse, who was run over by a horse and buggy in the street long before the Tampa Theatre was erected. Several other paranormal groups have sensed the presence of a man dressed in a Civil War–era uniform.

Plant Hall

The building that now houses Plant Hall at the University of Tampa was originally the Tampa Bay Hotel. The 511-room hotel was built between 1888 and 1891 by Henry B. Plant at a cost of $2.5 million. The architect, John A. Wood, designed the hotel in the Moorish Revival style complete with four cupolas, three domes, and six tall, slender towers called minarets. The Tampa Bay Hotel was noteworthy for having the first elevator ever installed in any building in Florida. In addition, the rooms were the first in any Florida hotel equipped with telephones and electric lights. Plant's penchant for extravagance extended to the grounds. The hotel's 150-acre site contained a casino, a golf course, a racetrack, a bowling alley, and a heated, indoor swimming pool.

In 1898 the hotel was used as a base of operations for the United States military. Colonel Teddy Roosevelt and his Rough Riders conducted maneuvers on the grounds. Famous guests included Babe Ruth, Clara Barton, Sarah Bernhardt, the Prince of Wales, and the Queen of England. After Henry Plant died in 1899 at the age of eighty, the hotel was run by his widow, Margaret, and their son, Morton. They later sold the building for $125,000 to the city of Tampa, which operated the hotel until 1930. The building stood empty for three years until late 1933, when Tampa Junior College converted the rooms and suites into offices and classrooms. After college became the University of Tampa, the administration agreed to maintain the historical integrity of the former hotel. In 1941 the university signed a ninety-nine-year lease with the city of Tampa for one dollar per year. The southwest wing of the building was reserved for the Tampa Municipal Museum, which was renamed the Henry B. Plant Museum in 1974. The museum is filled with antiques from the old hotel, many of which were purchased by Henry and Margaret Plant on their trips abroad.

Many students and employees who spend time in the classrooms and offices of Plant Hall believe that ghostly vestiges of the past live in the old hotel. The primary spirit is known as the Brown Man, who could be the ghost of Henry Plant. He is usually seen on the second floor of Plant Hall. One morning at 5:30, a female student entered the campus mailroom with her father, who worked there. After a while, she left the mailroom and proceeded to the second floor landing, where she saw a man in an old-fashioned, three-piece brown suit, standing about three hundred feet away. She asked him if he needed help. When he didn't respond, she walked close enough to see that he had glowing red eyes. She turned and ran back to the mailroom as fast as she could. A few weeks later, another student was in the same area when she saw a man in a brown suit standing in a corner, drinking what appeared to be a glass of tea. After a few seconds, he disappeared.

Security guards have also had bizarre experiences inside the old building. One officer set his coat on a chair, turned around for a few seconds, and looked back to find the coat on a different chair. Another security guard was doing a walk-through of Plant Hall late at night, making sure all of the doors were locked. As he was turning the doorknob to one of the offices, he felt as if someone was turning it in the opposite direction from the other side. A few seconds later, his flashlight was knocked out of his hand by what he described as an invisible force.

High levels of paranormal activity have also been reported in the science wing, which used to be the servants' quarters. People have heard the squeaky wheels of serving carts moving down the hallway. The ghost of a former caretaker is still on duty as well. Students have seen an elderly black man in a straw hat and boots in the science wing.

Falk Theatre

When the one-thousand-seat David Falk Theatre was built in 1928, it served primarily as a vaudeville stage. Touring companies of actors and actresses, jugglers, singers, and musicians performed at what was then known as the Park Theater. In the 1940s, the Falk Theatre was operated by Paramount Pictures through its subsidiary, E. J. Sparks, and in the early 1950s, it was owned by the Wometco Theater chain. The University of Tampa has owned the theater since 1962, and students enrolled in the school's musical theater program participate in stage productions and dance events.

In 1932, shortly before the Park Theater was converted to a movie house, actress Bessie Snavely discovered not only that her husband had been cheating on her with another actress but that he had run off with her as well. Consumed with rage and grief, Bessie at first considered killing him. Instead, she retired to her third-floor dressing room and hanged herself.

Bessie Snavely is remembered more today for her spectral appearances than for her stage appearances. Not long after her suicide, sightings of her ghost became a fairly regular occurrence, usually in her dressing room. Many people have reported walking through cold spots in the dressing room, and others have had the uneasy feeling that they were being watched. Some employees avoid entering the room altogether.

Some of the disturbances have been much more dramatic. In his book *Haunting Sunshine*, author Jack Powell says that a theater professor was standing in Bessie's dressing room one evening when several dressing room doors slammed shut in rapid succession. Michael Staczar, the chair of the University of Tampa's speech, theater, and dance department, was sitting in his office one afternoon in 1992 when he heard a loud pounding sound outside his door. When he opened the door, he saw the misty outline of a person that melted into the wall.

Bessie is perceived by staff members and students as a protective spirit and not a malevolent one. An employee was standing on a scaffold one day when he lost his balance. Just before he fell off, someone—or something—grabbed him from behind and helped him regain his footing. Bessie isn't benevolent all the time, however. Some people believe she has an intense aversion to the color red. Red costumes have turned up mutilated. One night the lead actress in a stage production was prevented from walking onstage by a pair of invisible hands. She was wearing a red dress at the time.

Still, students and staff have warm feelings for the theater ghost. For many years, a plaque honoring Bessie hung on a wall in her dressing room until it was stolen by students. So far, Bessie's ghost hasn't expressed her displeasure at the theft of her plaque.

The Bigelow-Helms House

Silas L. Bigelow was born on December 12, 1841, in Brooklyn, New York, to Johan and Martha Bigelow. He attended public school until he was fourteen and then worked as a clerk in a variety of businesses for the next six years. Between 1861 and 1865, Bigelow was a clerk in the quartermaster department of the 18th Army Corps. He spent the next eighteen years out

West working for railroad and express companies. In 1884 Bigelow moved to Tampa, where he secured employment as a merchant and real estate agent. In 1890 he set up the wholesale grain firm of Ross & Bigelow. He soon became one of Tampa's most prominent businessmen as well as one of the first members of the city council.

Bigelow and his wife, Mary, had four children, and in 1908 Bigelow built a mansion at 4807 Bayshore Boulevard to accommodate his large family. Built in the prairie style made popular by Frank Lloyd Wright, the house had a low hip roof and flared eaves. The walls were constructed of concrete blocks made to resemble rusticated stone. Bigelow died on April 22, 1913. In his obituary, his death was attributed to a heart attack. However, according to Bigelow Society Genealogy, he took his own life. At the time of his death, Bigelow was secretary of the Ybor City Land and Improvement Company and secretary of the Ybor City Building and Loan.

Records from the early twentieth century indicate that in 1917 or 1919, Bigelow's widow sold the mansion to Dr. John Sullivan Helms, who converted it into Bayside Hospital. Even though Dr. Helms added a wing to the west side of the old house in 1920, it still wasn't large enough to accommodate the growing number of patients. In 1927 the Tampa Municipal Hospital was constructed, and the Bigelow mansion became Dr. Helms' private residence. The added wing was demolished sometime between 1927 and 1930. A cousin of Dr. Helms, artist Jack Bonaker Wilson, lived in the attic and had his studio in the mansion. Members of the Helms family lived in the mansion until 1974. For a while, the house served as a catering hall and then stood vacant. In the early 1980s, the Borel Saladin family of Perroy, Switzerland, purchased the mansion and restored it.

Rumors that the Bigelow-Helms House might be haunted began circulating even before the mansion stood empty. People who lived and worked in the house reporting seeing the ghost of Silas Bigelow. The cries of babies were heard in empty rooms. Many people felt as if they were being watched by an invisible presence. Before the Saladin family bought the house, the walls were covered with blood and satanic symbols. Before the new owners moved in, they brought in a priest to bless the house.

Today the Bigelow-Helms House is used primarily as office space. Visitors still report seeing spectral figures standing in the hallways, and the cries of babies still echo through the house occasionally. The Bigelow-Helms House, it seems, is having a difficult time outliving its ghostly past.

Chapter Nineteen

Venice

Venice Theatre

The Venice Little Theatre opened in 1950 in a converted hangar at Venice Airport. Attendance grew steadily, and by the 1956–57 season, total attendance was 1,440 patrons. In 1972 the theater purchased one of the city's original 1926 buildings, the former gymnasium of the Kentucky Military Institute. The 286-seat theater continued to grow over the next few decades. By 1993 more than twenty thousand tickets were purchased. Renovation of the theater began in 1993 and continued through 1995. In 1996 the theater was expanded to 358 seats, and in 2000 a four-phase renovation project was completed at a cost more than $2 million. A $750,000 grant from the city of Venice and local foundations enabled the theater to purchase an adjacent building and parking lot. In 2008 the theater's board members changed its name to Venice Theatre to show that it had outgrown its "little" status. In 2010 and 2014, the Venice Theatre hosted the AACT International Community Theatre Festival.

Although the Venice Theatre has left its struggles far behind, a few ghostly remnants of the early years still remain. Staff members have reported hearing "spooky noises" at night, such as spectral footsteps and strange squeaking noises. For several nights in a row, witnesses reported seeing an eerie white light floating around the theater. According to Kim Cool, author of *Ghost Stories of Venice Old & New*, the first actual sighting in the theater occurred in 2006, when one of the actors rehearsing for a production of *Tom Sawyer* reported seeing the ghost of a little girl in the paint room. A few days later, the apparition appeared to two other young actors. The identity of the little ghost is unknown.

Works Cited

Books

Belanger, Jeff. *Ghosts of War*. Franklin Lakes, NJ: New Page Books, 2007.

Brown, Alan. *Haunted Pensacola*. Charleston, SC: History Press, 2010.

Cool, Kim. *Ghost Stories of Sarasota*. Venice, FL: Historic Venice Press, 2003.

_____. *Ghost Stories of Tampa Bay*. Venice, FL: Historic Venice Press, 2007.

_____. *Ghost Stories of Venice Old & New*. Venice, FL: Historic Venice Press, 2008.

Frethem, Deborah. *Ghost Stories of St. Petersburg, Clearwater and Pinellas County*. Charleston, SC: History Press, 2010.

Haskins, Lola. *Fifteen Florida Cemeteries*. Tallahassee, FL: University Press of Florida, 2011.

Hauck, Dennis William. *Haunted Places: The National Directory*. New York: Penguin, 1996.

Jenkins, Greg. *Florida's Ghostly Legends and Haunted Folklore*. 3 vols. Sarasota, FL: Pineapple Press, 2005–07.

Johnson, Sandra, and Leora Sutton. *Ghosts, Legends and Folklore of Old Pensacola*. Pensacola: Pensacola Historical Society, 1990.

Jones, Ray. *Haunted Lighthouses*. Guilford, CT. Globe Pequot Press, 2010.

Lewis, Chad, and Terry Fisk. *The Florida Road Guide to Haunted Locations*. Eau Claire, WI: Unexplained Research Publishing Company, 2010.

Moore, Joyce Elson. *Haunt Hunter's Guide to Florida*. Sarasota, FL: Pineapple Press, 1998.

Norman, Michael, and Beth Scott. *Historic Haunted America*. New York: TOR, 1995.

Powell, Jack. *Haunting Sunshine*. Sarasota, FL: Pineapple Press, 2001.

Reeser, Tim. *Ghost Stories of Tampa, Florida*. St. Petersburg, FL: 1stSight Press, 2007.

Sloan, David L. *Ghosts of Key West*. Key West, FL: Phantom Press, 1998.

Taylor, Troy. *The Ghost Hunter's Handbook*. Alton, IL: Whitechapel Press, 2001.

Winer, Richard, and Nancy Osborn. *Haunted Houses*. New York: Bantam, 1979.

Websites

A Virtual History of St. Petersburg, Florida: "The Famous & The Infamous: Some of St. Petersburg's Connections to the Notorious." http://virtual-explorations.org/infamous.htm

Angels & Ghosts. "Ghost Tours of the Southern U.S." http://angelsghosts.com/ghost_tours_south.html

Angels & Ghosts. "Key West Cemetery Ghost Pictures." http://www.angelsghosts. com/key_west_cemetery_ghost_pictures.html

Audubon House & Tropical Gardens. http://www.audubonhouse.com

Bryant, Charles W., and Jessika Toothman. "Top 10 Hotels That Will Scare the Daylights Out of You." http://science.howstuffworks.com/science-myth-vs-myth/afterlife/top-5-haunted-hotels.htm

Burroughs Home & Gardens. "History." http://www.burroughshome.com/history/

Ceprofs.civil.tamu.edu. "The Approach" and "The Storm." https://ceprofs.civil.tamu.edu/llowery/personal/songs/hurricane/thestorm/approach.htm

Coastal Breeze News. "The Legend of the Pirate Gasparilla." http://www.coastalbreezenews.com/2010/03/26/the-legend-of-the-pirate-gasparilla/

Conlon, Sean. "Haunted Ghost Stories in Ybor City and Tampa." http://www.813area.com/entertainment/haunted-ghost-stories-in-ybor-city-and-tampa.html

Cracker Barrel. "Heritage & History." http://www.crackerbarrel.com/about-us/heritage-and-history

Crowne Plaza Hotels & Resorts. "La Concha Key West Hotel

Welcomes You to Key West Florida!" http://www.
crowneplaza.com/hotels/us/en/key-west/eywlc/
hoteldetail?sicontent=0&sicreat

DeNote, Mark. Cigar City Brewing. "Tampa Brewing History."
http://cigarcitybrewing.com/tampa-bay-brewing-
history/

Egmont Key Lighthouse. "Egmont Key Lighthouse and More."
http://www.egmontkeylighthouse.com/

Exploring Florida. "Tocobaga Indians of Tampa Bay." http://
fcit.usf.edu/florida/lessons/tocobag/tocobag1.htm

Flori de Leon Apartments, Inc. "About the Flori." http://www.
florideleon.org/?page_id=183

Florida Studio Theatre. "About FST." http://www.
floridastudiotheatre.org/about.php

Fort DeSoto Park. "Fort Construction." http://www.fortdesoto.
com/fortconstruction.php

Fort Myers Florida Weekly. "Ghost tracking group finds haunts
in Fort Myers." http://fortmyers.floridaweekly.com/
news/2007-04-12/Top_News/Ghost_tracking_group_
finds_haunts_in_Fort_Myers.html

Fort Myers Florida Weekly. "Ghostly tales to be told at
Burroughs Home." http://fortmyers.floridaweekly.com/
news/2011-10-19/Arts_(and)_Entertainment_News/
Ghostly_tales_to_be_told_at_Burroughs_Home.html

Fort Zachary Taylor State Park. "History." http://www.
fortzacharytaylor.com/history.html

Ghost Stories. "The Tampa Theatre." http://paranormalstories.
blogspot.com/2009/11/tampa-theatre.html

Ghost Towns. "Fort Pickens." http://www.ghosttowns.com/
states/fl/fortpickens.html

Ghosts & Gravestones. "Key West Ghost Stories." http://www.
ghostsandgravestones.com/key-west/ghost-tour-tales.
htm

Ghosts of America. "Gulf Shores, Alabama Ghost Sightings."
http://ghostsofamerica.com/3/Alabama_Gulf_Shores_
ghost_sightings.html

Hard Rock Café. "Hard Rock Café: Key West." http://
www.hardrock.com/locations/cafes3/cafe.
aspx?LocationID=90&MIBenumID=3

Harry S. Truman Little White House. "Truman Little White
House Key West Museum History." http://www.

trumanlittlewhitehouse.com/key-west/history-little-white-house-museum.htm

Harry S. Truman Little White House. "Welcome to the Harry S. Truman Little White House." http://www.trumanlittlewhitehouse.com/

Haunted Baseball. "Preview Chapter: Stompin' at the Vinoy." http://www.hauntedbaseball.com/preview.html

Haunted Houses. "Hemingway House." http://www.hauntedhouses.com/states/fl/hemingway-house.htm

Haunted Hovel. "The Vinoy Hotel, St. Petersburg." http://www.hauntedhovel.com/vinoyhotel.html

Haunted Places to Go. "The Haunted Florida Renaissance Vinoy Resort in St. Petersburg." http://www.haunted-places-to-go.com/haunted-florida.html

Haunting America. "Cuban Club." http://hauntingamerica.com/cuban-club/

Historic Key West Inns. "Cypress House." http://www.historickeywestinns.com/the-Inns/cypress-house/

Historical Marker Database. "Landes-McDonough House." http://www.hmdb.org/marker.asp?marker=50048

Hotel News Resource. "After 75 Years a Ritz-Carlton Hotel Is Scheduled to Open Today in Sarasota, Florida." http://www.hotelnewsresource.com/article4007

Hub Pages. "Haunted Key West." http://crazyhorsesghost.hubpages.com/hub/Haunted-Key-West

Hub Pages. "Haunted Ybor City in Tampa, FL: A Murderer's Ghost and Other Specters." http://kittythedreamer.hubpages.com/hub/The-Hauntings-of-Ybor-City

Island Hotel & Restaurant. "The History of the Island Hotel." http://islandhotel-cedarkey.com/history.html

Key West Art & Historical Society. "Fort East Martello." http://www.kwahs.com/martello.htm

Key West Attractions Association. "Audubon House." http://www.keywestattractions.org/audubon-house-museum.php

Key West Ghosts. "Audubon House and Gardens." http://www.keywestparanormal.com/Locations/AudubonHouse.html

_____. "Banyan Resort and Guesthouse." http://www.keywestparanormal.com/Locations/BanyanResortandGuesthouse.html

_____. "Captain Tony's Saloon." http://www.

keywestparanormal.com/Locations/
CaptainTonysSaloon.html

_____. "Chelsea House Pool and Gardens." http://www.
keywestparanormal.com/Locations/ChelseaHouse.html

_____. Crowne Plaza La Concha Hotel." http://
www.keywestparanormal.com/Locations/
CrownePlazaLaConchaHotel.html

_____. "Fort Zachary Taylor." http://www.keywestparanormal.
com/Locations/FortZacharyTaylor.html

_____. "Hard Rock Café." http://www.keywestparanormal.
com/Locations/HardRockCafe.html

_____. "Hemingway House." http://www.keywestparanormal.
com/Locations/HemingwayHouse.html

_____. "Key West Cemetery." http://www.keywestparanormal.
com/Locations/KeyWestCemetery.html

_____. "Old Town Manor (Eaton Lodge)." http://www.
keywestparanormal.com/Locations/EatonLodge.html

_____. "St. Paul's Episcopal Church Cemetery." http://
www.keywestparanormal.com/Locations/
StPaulsEpiscopalChurch.html

Kruse, Michael. "St. Petersburg's Vinoy hotel haunted, major-
league baseball players
say." http://www.sdparanormal.com/articles/
article/1961531/163512.htm

Lighthouse Friends. "Egmont Key, FL." http://www.
lighthousefriends.com/light.asp?ID=370

_____. "Pensacola, FL." http://www.lighthousefriends.com/
light.asp?ID=589

Mayo, Loren. "The Observer hunts ghosts at The Players
Theatre."
http://www.yourobserver.com/news/sarasota/Front-
Page/1027201114971/The-Observer-hunts-ghosts-at-
The-Players-Theatre

McDonald, Tim. "Renaissance Vinoy Resort & Golf Club has
Marilyn Monroe, ghosts galore and tight fairways."
http://www.worldgolf.com/course-reviews/florida/
renaissance-resort-vinoy-golf-club-st-petersburg-
florida-9000.htm

Moore, David. "Pensacola Lighthouse: A Real Haunted
Lighthouse."
http://information-spirituality.blogspot.com/2008/08/
pensacola-lighthouse-real-haunted.html

Morgan, Kimberly. "Pirate Ghosts of Tampa Bay." http://voices.
      yahoo.com/pirate-ghosts-tampa-bay-10226363.html

Most Haunted Places in America. "Haunted Cedar Keys Island
      Hotel." http://www.ghosteyes.com/haunted-cedar-keys-
      island-hotel

_____. "'The Captain' at the Royalty Theater." http://www.
      ghosteyes.com/captain-royalty-theater

_____. "The Hauntings of the Provincial Hotel." http://www.
      ghosteyes.com/hauntings-provincial-hotel

National Park Service. "Fort Pickens." http://www.nps.gov/
      guis/planyourvisit/fort-pickens.htm

Old Town Manor. http://www.oldtownmanor.com

Peace River Ghost Tracker. "Pullman train the Esperanza:
      Lee county historical society." http://www.
      peaceriverghosttracker.com/subPages2/esperanza.htm.

Pensapedia. "Tivoli High House." http://pensapedia.com/wiki/
      Tivoli_High_House

_____. "Tower East." http://www.pensapedia.com/wiki/Tower_
      East

Perkins, Robert E. "The First Fifty Years – Ringling School of
      Art and Design: 1931–1981." http://www.ringling.edu/
      fileadmin/pdf/TheFirst50Years.pdf.

Pollock, Angie. "Haunted Destinations: The Dorr House in
      Pensacola Fla."
      http://www.travelersguide360.com/index.php/haunted-
      destinations-the-dorr-house-in-pensacola-fla-15183/

PSIresearcher. "St. Pete High School at Mirror Lake: A
      Little School Spirit." http://psiresearcher.wordpress.
      com/2012/03/05/st-pete-high-school-at-mirror-lake-a-
      little-spirit/

_____. "The Case of the Haunted Cracker Barrel Restaurant."
      http://psiresearcher.wordpress.com/?s=cracker+barrel

_____. "The Ringling School of Art and Design and a
      ghost named Mary." http://psiresearcher.wordpress.
      com/2011/10/28/the-ringling-school-of-art-and-design

_____. "The Vinoy Hotel and a Lady in White." http://
      psiresearcher.wordpress.com/2012/03/16/the-vinoy-
      hotel-and-a-lady-in-white/

Research and Investigations of the Paranormal/R.I.P.
      Hunters. "Investigate the Historic Royal Theater in

Clearwater Fla." http://www.meetup.com/riphunters/
    events/17546195/
Ringling College of Art and Design. "About." http://www.
    ringling.edu/about/
Safety Harbor Resort and Spa. "Resort History." http://www.
    safetyharborspa.com/history/history.html
Sarasota Opera. "Theater History." http://www.sarasotaopera.
    org/about/theater_history.aspx
Seville Quarter. "A Pensacola Tradition Since 1967." http://
    www.sevillequarter.com/history
Shoestring Weekends. "Key West's Hard Rock Café."
    http://shoestringweekends.wordpress.com/tag/hard-
    rock-cafe/
_____. "One of America's Most Haunted Rooms!" http://
    shoestringweekends.wordpress.com/2012/09/24/most/
Smith, Mark D. Journals of Yesteryear. "Ringling's Ritz-
    Carlton: Dream Withers with Boom's End."   http://
    www.sarasotahistoryalive.com/stories/journals-of-
    yesteryear/ringling-s-ritz-carlton/
Southern Spirit Guide. "Vinoy, Women and Song—
    Vinoy Renaissance Hotel (Haunt Brief)." http://
    southernspiritguide.blogspot.com/2012/03/vinoy-
    women-and-songvinoy-renaissance.html
St. Paul's Episcopal Church. "History." http://stpaulskeywest.
    org/History.html
Starkimages.homestead.com. "Safety Harbor Spa." http://
    starkimages.homestead.com/safetyharborspa.html
Tampa Bay Times. "Clearwater negotiating to buy old Royalty
    Theatre building."
    http://www.tampabay.com/news/localgovernment/
    article838940.ece
_____. "Couple buys 80-year-old penthouse of Babe Ruth."
    http://www.tampabay.com/news/business/realestate/
    article955390.ece
_____. "St. Pete's Vinoy Resort appears on Sci Fi Channel's
    Ghost Hunters series Wednesday." http://www.
    tampabay.com/blogs/media/content/st-petes-vinoy-
    resort-appears-sci-fi-channels-ghost-hunters-series-
    wednesday/2095119
Tampa Ghost Watchers. "The Haunted Skyway Bridge
    in Florida." http://tampaghostwatchers.blogspot.
    com/2007/11/good-article.html

The Artist House. "History." http://www.artisthousekeywest.
    com/about/key-west-hotel-history/

The Columns Hotel. "About Us." http://www.thecolumns.com/
    about.htm#!about/cjn9

The Ernest Hemingway Home & Museum. "Hemingway: The
    Legend." http://www.hemingwayhome.com/legend/

The Expressionist. "A Sacred Land." http://www.
    theexpressionist.com/tag/boca-ciega-bay

The Players. "About." http://theplayers.org/index.php/about-2/

The Skeptical Viewer. "GH: Renaissance Vinoy Resort." http://
    www.skepticalviewer.com/2008/10/06/gh-renaissance-
    vinoy-resort/

The Witching Hour. "Haunted Lodgings: Don Cesar Beach
    Resort – St. Petersburg, FL." http://4girlsandaghost.
    wordpress.com/2011/01/27/haunted-lodgings-don-
    cesar-beach-resort-st-petersburg-fl

TopTenz. "Top 10 Most Haunted Cities in the U.S." http://www.
    toptenz.net/Top-10-most-haunted-cities-in-the-u-s.
    php

True Hauntings of America. "The Haunting of Fort Gaines."
    http://hauntsofamerica.blogspot.com/2007/08/
    haunting-of-fort-gaines.html

Vanhoose, Joe. Ocala Star Banner. "'Ghost Hunters' drawn to
    Ocala inn." http://www.ocala.com/article/20080930/
    NEWS/809290364

Venice Theatre. "History." http://venicestage.com/about-
    venice-theatre/history/

Virtual Tourist. "Cemetery and Ghosts, Key West."
    http://www.virtualtourist.com/travel/North_America/
    United_States_of_America/Florida/Key_West-763140/
    Off_the_Beaten_Path-Key_West-Cemetery_and_
    Ghosts-BR-1.html

Virtual Tourist. "The Ghosts of Tampa." http://members.
    virtualtourist.com/m/tt/69f69

Visit Pensacola. "Quayside Art Gallery/Pensacola Artists, Inc."
    http://www.visitpensacola.com/listings/%5Blist_
    id%5D-275

Waymarking.com. "Cracker Barrel haunting – Naples, FL."
    http://www.waymarking.com/waymarks/WM4KEW_
    Cracker_Barrel_Haunting_Naples_FL

_____. "Vinoy Hotel – St. Petersburg, FL." http://www.
waymarking.com/waymarks/WM5NNY_Vinoy_
Hotel_St_Petersburg_FL

Welcome to Sacred Lands. http://www.jungleprada.blogspot.
com/

Where. "Cypress House Guest Studios." http://www.
wheretraveler.com/key-west/cypress-house-guest-
studios

Wikipedia. "Captain Tony's Saloon." http://en.wikipedia.org/
wiki/Captain_Tony%27s_Saloon

_____. "Egmont Key Light." http://en.wikipedia.org/wiki/
Egmont_Key_Lighthouse

_____. "Egmont Key State Park." http://en.wikipedia.org/wiki/
Egmont_Key_State_Park

_____. "Ernest Hemingway." http://en.wikipedia.org/wiki/
Ernest_Hemingway

_____. "Fort Pickens." http://en.wikipedia.org/wiki/Fort_
Pickens

_____. "Harry S. Truman Little White House." http://
en.wikipedia.org/wiki/Harry_S._Truman_Little_
White_House

_____. "Jose Gaspar." http://en.wikipedia.org/wiki/
Jos%C3%A9_Gaspar

_____. "Key West Cemetery." http://en.wikipedia.org/wiki/
Key_West_Cemetery

_____. "Murphy-Burroughs House." http://en.wikipedia.org/
wiki/Murphy-Burroughs_House

_____. "Ringling College of Art and Design." http://
en.wikipedia.org/wiki/
Ringling_College_of_Art_and_Design

_____. "St. Petersburg High School." http://en.wikipedia.org/
wiki/St._Petersburg_High_School

_____. "Sarasota Opera House." http://en.wikipedia.org/wiki/
Sarasota_Opera_House

Wilson Plaza. "Wilson Plaza History." http://www.wilsonplaza.
com/about.php

Woods, Amanda. Travel Tales. "Haunted Key West Hotels to
Stay in or Avoid." http://amanda-woods.suite101.com/
haunted-key-west-hotels-to-stay-in-or-avoid-a168195

Ybor Chamber. "Cuban Club." http://www.ybor.org/cuban_
club

Zucco, Tom. "Hunt for haunts." http://www.sptimes.
        com/2002/10/31/TampaBay/Hunt_for_haunts.shtml
Zuko.com. Haunted Cemeteries and Graveyards. "St. Paul's
        Episcopal Church Graveyard." http://www.zuko.com/
        CrypticSphere/Haunted_Graveyards_Key_West.asp
_____. Haunted Cemeteries and Graveyards. "The Key West
        Cemetery." http://www.zuko.com/CrypticSphere/
        Haunted_Key_West_Cemetery.asp

Interviews

Coleman, Eddie. Personal interview. September 18, 2012.

Lewis, Trent. Personal interview. September 12, 2012.

Sutton, Sharon. Personal interview. July 30, 2012.

Valdes, Richard. Personal interview. September 24, 2012.